MW00929747

What Teachers, Parents and Students are Saying about

MARKED EVIDENCE

"It's fun to read a book that includes places that my students will be familiar with. It's an interesting mystery of which young readers can learn from the perseverance of the teenagers in the story. I like their unselfish attitude as they give up what is left of their summer to help their aunt. More than that, the dialogue, setting, and events are very realistic and true to the young Colorado reader."

Eileen Heath
3rd Grade Teacher
Tavelli Elementary School, Ft. Collins, CO

"Emily Burns has found her calling; her new Rocky Mountain Mystery Series is exciting to read and realistic. I found it very refreshing that her book portrays traditional families with good moral values. In reading her third book, Marked Evidence, I found it hard to put down, I wanted to read on and find out what her characters would uncover next! Her inclusion of local landmarks is wonderful. Some of our teachers have discussed using her books in their Colorado History curriculum. I can't wait to put all three of her books in my library."

Laurel Enslen
Librarian, Singing Hills Elementary, Parker, CO

More of What People are Saying

"It was exciting to come across names of familiar places in Ft. Collins and Colorado. The story flowed smoothly and had an intriguing conclusion."

Diana Chastain
4th Grade Teacher
Poudre School District, Ft. Collins

"Marked Evidence is a fast paced mystery that entertains as well as teaches. The mix of local Colorado history and locations makes the book especially interesting and personal for anyone who has ever lived in or visited one of Colorado's Front Range cities. Marked Evidence is easy to read but provides enough challenge for its intended audience to keep them interested and engaged from start to finish."

Heather Clark
Colorado Welcome Center

"It's a mind boggling mystery with lots of twists and turns."

Shelby - 9 years old.

"You never know what will happen next."

Jeremy - 10 years old.

"I really enjoyed making pictures in my head as the adventures of the mystery unfolded."

Emma - 9 years old.

"This book brought my imagination alive."

Hanna - 9 years old.

"This book is so exciting that we never wanted to put it down."

Brennan - 9 years old.

Rocky Mountain Mysteries™

MARKED EVIDENCE

Emily Burns

Illustrated By
John Breeding

Covered Wagon Publishing LLC

ROCKY MOUNTAIN MYSTERIES: 3
    MARKED EVIDENCE

ISBN: 0-9723259-2-1

10 9 8 7 6 5 4 3 2 First Printing: March 2003

Printed in the United States of America by:
    Color House Graphics
    3505 Eastern S. E. · Grand Rapids, MI 49508
    Cover printed on 10PT C1S- Bright white cover with lay-flat gloss laminate.
    Interior pages printed on 60$^{\#}$ White Smooth Offset

Published and distributed by

    Covered Wagon Publishing, LLC,
    PO Box 473038 Aurora, Colorado 80047-3038.
    jackd@coveredwagonpublishing.com

Library of Congress Control Number: 2003101231

Illustrated by John Breeding

Book Design, Cover Design and Art Direction by

A. J. Images Inc.
Communication & Graphic Design
www.ajimagesinc.com – 303•696•9227

For educational and individual sales information,
call Covered Wagon Publishing, 1.303.751.0992
Visit our web site at: http://www.RockyMountainMysteries.com

Acknowledgements

We would like to thank everyone
who has contributed to the success of
the Rocky Mountain Mystery series
with a very special thanks to the many teachers
who have supported this venture.

A thanks also goes out to all of the businesses
that gave us permission to use their names
in this book. Among them are:
Six Flag Elitch Gardens, the Colorado Rockies,
and Alpine Funtier.

Lastly, thanks to all of the kids
who enjoy reading the books
and look forward to reading
the next book in the series.

Dedicated to Tyler, Dylan, Andrew,
Kamryn, Lee, Adam, Michael,
and Stephanie, all of whom have contributed
in my strong desire to succeed.

Tyler -

is sixteen years old and has brown hair and brown eyes. His hobbies include camping, fishing, baseball, and white water rafting. His best friend is Dylan.

Dylan -

is sixteen years old with reddish/brown hair. He is on the high school football team and enjoys fishing, watching movies, and hanging out with his friends.

Stephanie -

is fourteen years old and a twin to her brother, Steve. She enjoys reading, writing, and playing the piano. Stephanie's best friend is Kamryn.

Kamryn -

is thirteen years old with blond hair and blue eyes. Her hobbies include shopping, music, reading, the drama club, playing games, and bike riding.

Steve -

has light brown hair and hazel eyes like his twin sister. His favorite pastime is baseball. He enjoys reading, camping, photography, and fishing. His best friend is Andrew.

Andrew -

is thirteen years old with brown hair and brown eyes. His hobbies include wrestling, baseball, swimming, and collecting trading cards.

Contents

Chapter 1
Tricked

As the Thompson family walked in the door, the phone was ringing. Jack Thompson answered it and informed the others that it was his sister, Michele, calling.

"Is anything wrong, Jack?" Carol Thompson asked her husband. She knew that it wasn't like his sister to call so late in the evening.

Jack motioned for her to be quiet and then said, "Why, that's terrible, Sis."

As Jack talked with Michele, he learned that his sister's entire inventory for her new antique store had been stolen. Luckily, all of it was insured and she expected an insurance check to cover her lost antiques. Unfortunately, it had taken a lot of time to find the original pieces for her store, and now it would be impossible for her to open the new store on time without some help.

"Carol and I would be happy to help, but we were just assigned a series of articles about the Old West Trail, and we have to meet a tight deadline," Jack Thompson told his sister.

The Thompsons had recently become professional travel writers after Jack had spent several years teaching history and Carol had sold real estate.

"We can help her, Dad," fourteen-year-old Stephanie volunteered.

"That's a great idea," Stephanie's twin brother, Steve, agreed.

"And we'll get to spend some time with Michael," Tyler said referring to their ten-year-old cousin.

"I think I have some volunteers right here. I'll let you talk to the head honcho," Jack Thompson said, handing the receiver over to his oldest son, Tyler.

Tyler was sixteen and had a driver's license. It had come in handy when the teenagers spent the beginning of the summer with their Aunt Marybeth solving the mystery, <u>Manitou Art Caper</u>.

After hanging up the phone, Tyler informed everyone that he had told their aunt that they would drive up the following day after church.

"That's fine but I think I better drive you kids," Mr. Thompson told his son. "Fort Collins is a good four hours away and too far for you to drive by yourself."

"Oh, Dad," Tyler started to complain.

"What if Dad follows us?" Stephanie quickly suggested.

"Yeah, that way we will have a vehicle to use while we're there," Steve said.

"And the truck will come in handy in hauling antiques," Tyler added.

"Okay, okay," Jack Thompson, said laughing. "You kids all think alike."

Excitedly, the teenagers headed upstairs to their bedrooms to pack. Once upstairs Steve was the first to suggest that maybe they could catch the thieves.

"Yeah, it sounds like we have another mystery to solve," Stephanie agreed.

"Unfortunately, it means that we will have to cancel our plans with our friends this week," Steve said.

"That's right, Kamryn and I were going to the mall, and..." Stephanie started to say.

"Who cares about the mall," her brother interrupted her. "Andrew's father was taking us on an all-day fishing trip on Wednesday."

"I am sure that Mr. Phillips will take you fishing another time," Tyler said. "Let's drive over and tell Andrew and Dylan the news."

While Steve was best friends with Andrew, Tyler was best friends with Andrew's older brother Dylan so it was easy to tell both of them about their change of plans. Tyler also had a favor to ask Dylan. He had just recently become a Big Brother to a younger kid who needed a friend and he was hoping that Dylan could help fill in while he was gone.

"I promised Bobby that I would take him to the movies tomorrow," he explained.

"Sure, I don't mind taking him, and luckily we've already met so I won't be a total stranger," Dylan said. "How long do you think you'll be in Fort Collins?"

"I have no idea," Tyler said. "It sounds like Aunt Michele really needs our help."

"Well, good luck and I'll spend some time with Bobby," Dylan said.

"Thanks, I really owe you one," Tyler said as he waved good-bye.

Sunday morning the Thompson family was up early for a big breakfast before church. After the service, the family headed back to the Thompson house where they had a quick lunch before heading to Aunt Michele's house. It had been decided that Tyler's parents would follow him into Fort Collins, and from there the Thompsons would continue their drive into Wyoming to start researching their next assignment.

"We'll be following you all the way into Fort Collins but then you'll need to take Hwy 14," Jack Thompson told his son.

"Right, I know how to get to Aunt Michele's from there," Tyler replied. "And we have her phone number just in case."

"And call us on our cell phone as soon as you arrive," Carol Thompson said.

"We will, don't worry, Mom," Steve told his mother.

The teenagers said good-bye to their parents and Tyler started their father's truck. They couldn't wait to get to their aunt's so they could begin their investigation.

Reaching the town of Fort Collins, Tyler took the exit for Hwy 14 and the kids waved good-bye to their parents.

He followed the winding road and then took a right onto College Avenue. When he came to Bear Canyon Road he took another right, and a few minutes later they pulled into Aunt Michele's driveway.

"Hey guys, it's good to see you," Michael said, greeting them. "I'm glad that you can help Mom and me."

"It'll be fun," Steve said, hugging his cousin.

Aunt Michele was just as happy to see the teenagers.

"I just took some chocolate chip cookies out of the oven," she told them. "Would you like some?"

The teenagers were helping themselves to the cookies when Stephanie remembered that they needed to call their parents.

"Oh, and Dad said to give this money to you so that we are no bother," Tyler said handing his aunt an envelope.

"What bother?" Aunt Michele said. "I need the help."

After phoning their parents, Aunt Michele showed them the section of her house where she planned to open her antique store, Mayfair Antiques. The front part of her house had an entryway, a large living room, and a smaller room, which at one time had been a parlor. Now she planned to use the space for her new store.

"How are you going to decorate the rooms?" Stephanie asked, hoping that her aunt didn't plan on leaving the faded and worn flowered wallpaper that was now covering the walls.

"I bought wallpaper to put up but now that I have to buy new inventory, I don't think I'll have time," Aunt Michele said.

"We can help you put it up," Tyler said.

"Yeah, we've helped Mom and Dad put up lots of wallpaper," Stephanie told her aunt. "Can we see what you picked out?"

"Sure," Aunt Michele replied as she left the room to get the wallpaper.

A few minutes later their aunt returned with a roll of wallpaper. It was decorated with little white, violet, and yellow flowers, and even though the design was with flowers, the boys even liked it.

"It looks like something that would go in an antique shop," Steve commented.

"Yeah, I love it," Stephanie agreed.

"Now all we need are some antiques to sell in the furniture shop," Michael said.

"Where did you get all of the antiques that you were planning to sell in the first place?" Stephanie asked.

"I got them from all over," she replied. "I went to a lot of auctions and estate sales and whenever I saw a good deal, I'd grab it."

"It sounds like we have our work cut out for us to find replacement furniture before your grand opening," Stephanie commented.

"It isn't going to be easy," their aunt said, frowning. "I have several places for us to try, starting with an estate sale first thing in the morning."

"Hopefully, we can at least find a few pieces to start your inventory," Tyler said.

"We can only pray," Aunt Michele said. "In the meantime, dinner is ready."

"This sure smells delicious. I didn't realize how hungry I was," Steve said as he helped himself to some of his aunt's meatloaf.

"You're always hungry," Stephanie teased her brother.

During dinner Aunt Michele explained that the furniture had been stored in her garage when it was stolen.

"When do you think it was stolen?" Tyler asked.

"Last Thursday Michael and I went out to dinner and returned to discover everything gone," Aunt Michele told them.

"Was it a late dinner?" Steve asked.

"No, it was an early dinner because we worked through lunch that day," she replied. "We left around 3 o'clock and were home before 5 o'clock."

"Then the furniture was stolen in broad daylight!" Steve said.

"That's right. I couldn't believe it as we pulled into the driveway. The garage door was left wide open and the garage was completely cleaned out," she said.

"And the police didn't find any clues when they came to investigate?" Tyler asked.

"No, the police only concluded that the side door to the garage was opened with a crowbar, and they did find some fingerprints," Aunt Michele added.

"Do they have any suspects?" Stephanie asked.

"No, they just called it a typical robbery and asked me if I had insurance," she said.

"It doesn't sound like there is much that the police can do," Steve said.

"No, and it's a shame how people can get away with these crimes," Aunt Michele commented.

"They are not going to get away with it if we can help it," Tyler said.

After dinner, the teenagers watched a movie with their aunt and cousin, and then made it an early night. The estate sale started at eight o'clock the next morning, and was in Denver, a good distance away.

The next morning the family arrived at the estate sale before anyone else. Unfortunately, they soon learned that there wasn't anything worth buying.

"It's always a matter of luck with these things," Aunt Michele said.

"Where should we go next?" Tyler asked.

"There are several antique stores nearby," their aunt replied. "I thought that we could visit a few and see if we can find any clearance sales."

But as the group tried one antique store after another, they discovered the same thing about each of them. Aunt Michele wouldn't make a profit if she paid the prices that they were charging.

The family had been to about half a dozen stores when Aunt Michele decided that she was finished with antique hunting for the day.

"We could visit a few more places, it's not even 1 o'clock yet," Tyler said, looking at his watch.

"Actually I think it's about time that we left for the park," their aunt said, smiling.

"What park?" Steve asked.

"Well, I wanted to take you kids to see a baseball

game but since the Rockies are out of town, I though we could go to Elitch's instead," she replied.

Elitch Gardens was a theme park that dated back over one hundred years. In 1995 the park relocated to the downtown Denver area and became America's only downtown theme park. Recently, the park had joined Six Flags to become Six Flags Elitch Gardens.

Everyone cheered at the idea. The theme park was so big that there was something that interested each of them. While the twins looked forward to the many water slides, Tyler was interested in riding the roller coasters and Michael wanted to see a stunt show.

"Well, we have all afternoon," Aunt Michele said, smiling. "But first I think we should have lunch."

"I'll second that," Steve said as they entered the theme park.

After grabbing a bite to eat, the teenagers wasted no time and started getting in line for various rides. With over forty to choose from, they each had their favorite. After several hours, the group was exhausted.

"You don't realize how hot it is outside until you spend most of the afternoon in the sun," Stephanie said.

"Yeah, I am definitely ready to head over to the other side the park where all of the water rides are," Steve said. "How about it, guys?"

Everyone quickly agreed and soon they were splashing in the water. The cool water definitely helped cool them off, but now the only problem was that they would have to ride all the way back to Aunt Michele's house in wet clothes. Luckily, their aunt had an old blanket that she always kept in the car for them to sit on.

"I'm glad you kids had fun," Aunt Michele said as they were leaving the park. "And it took my mind off this antique dilemma."

"Don't worry, we'll find some good deals," Michael told his mother.

"I know, Son," she replied and then added. "It's just going to take some time and I might have to change the date for my opening day."

Arriving back at Aunt Michele's house, things were starting to look brighter after she checked her voice mail messages.

"I have good news!" she told everyone. "It turns out that a store where I bought several items on clearance was planning on opening a second store but their plans fell through. They have a lot of merchandise to get rid of. They heard my story on the evening news and called to see if I might be interested in their extra furniture. It sounds like I can get some real bargains."

"That's super!" Michael said, hugging his mom.

Aunt Michele returned the phone call from Mr. Gomez to learn that they had several pieces of furniture that she was interested in purchasing.

"Mr. Gomez is going to send me an email with a list of his inventory and photographs of each item," Aunt Michele said after she hung up.

It was only minutes later when the email message appeared on Aunt Michele's computer.

"There are several items very similar to the ones that got stolen and a few of them are even cheaper than what I paid to begin with," Aunt Michele exclaimed after reading over the email.

"Steve and I can go pick up whatever items you decide on," Tyler volunteered.

"Are you sure, Tyler?" Aunt Michele asked.

"Sure, the only problem is that I don't know how much furniture I can haul in Dad's truck," Tyler said.

After Aunt Michele put together a list of items that she wanted, Tyler suggested that he rent a truck so that he could bring back everything in one trip.

"Actually, Brian, a friend of mine, who is also in the furniture business, has a large moving truck that he said we could borrow," Aunt Michele said. "I'll give him a call and find out when it would be a good time for us to borrow it."

After talking to her friend over the phone, Aunt Michele hung up and told them that they could pick up the truck anytime.

"Then, how about going right now?" Tyler asked. "That way Steve and I can drive up tomorrow morning to pick up the furniture that you want."

"Sounds good to me, but first I better call Mr. Gomez back and ask him to hold the furniture for me," Aunt Michele said.

After talking with Mr. Gomez, who agreed to hold the furniture, Aunt Michele and Tyler left to pick up the truck. Aunt Michele's friend, Brian, didn't live far away, and they returned shortly.

"We can move a lot of furniture using Brian's truck," Tyler told the others.

"And this time we are not storing it in the garage," Michael said.

"That's right, we better get the store ready," Aunt Michele said.

"I can help you put up the wallpaper while they are picking up the furniture," Stephanie told her aunt.

"That sounds like a plan," Aunt Michele agreed.

The following day Tyler and Steve drove down to Boulder to Sandra's Antiques where they were to pick up the furniture that Aunt Michele had put on hold. The managers had already set aside several pieces of furniture for them when they arrived.

"We have everything right here in this corner," said the manager, who had dark brown hair and spoke with an Hispanic accent. "We'll help you move it."

As they moved the furniture into the truck, they soon realized that even the moving truck wasn't big enough to carry it all. They would have to come back for a large cabinet and an old rocking chair.

Meanwhile, Stephanie and Michael helped Aunt Michele decorate what would soon be Mayfair Antiques. The wallpaper was very old so it didn't take much to remove it, but then they had to scrub the walls.

"I can't wait to start putting up the new wallpaper," Stephanie said.

Washing the walls didn't take long and soon they were putting up wallpaper. They were almost done when Tyler and Steve returned.

"The room looks great," Steve said, walking in the door.

"It sure does," Tyler agreed.

"We only have one more wall to wallpaper and then the room will be ready for the furniture," Stephanie said.

The boys helped put up the wallpaper while Aunt Michele made lunch.

"Lunch is on the table," she called to them.

"Sounds great, I'm starving!" Steve said.

"You're just wasting away," Stephanie said.

"Very funny," Steve answered back.

The family was eating lunch when a friend of Aunt Michele's dropped in. She introduced her friend, Bobbie and invited her to join them for lunch.

"No, thanks, I just stopped in to see how you were doing," Bobbie said.

Aunt Michele filled her friend in on the furniture that she had just bought.

"It sounds like things are looking up for you," Bobbie said. "I can't wait to see the furniture."

"Bobbie is an expert in antiques and has taught me a lot about them," Aunt Michele said.

"Well, I don't know about being called an expert," Bobbie said. "Let's see what you kids brought back."

As they started looking at the antiques, the teenagers immediately sensed that something was wrong.

"What's the matter?" Tyler asked.

"Something isn't right about this table," Aunt Michele said.

"You're right," Bobbie said. "It's only a reproduction."

"What do you mean?" Stephanie asked.

"Sometimes reproductions are not easy to spot but this table is definitely not authentic," Bobbie answered.

"Does that mean we brought back furniture that isn't worth what we paid?" Tyler asked.

"I'm afraid so," Bobbie answered with a sigh.

"We were swindled!" Tyler exclaimed.

Chapter 2
Vanished

"I can't believe that the store tricked us," Tyler said, after they realized that the antique store had sold them reproductions.

"They sold me beautiful antiques the first time I was there," Aunt Michele said.

"Maybe that one piece was just a fluke that the store bought off someone else," Tyler suggested.

But after some time examining the antiques, Aunt Michele and Bobbie both pointed out several flaws in many of the items. Examining underneath a dining room table it appeared that the leaves and base did not belong with the same table, as if the parts belonged to another table. On an old dresser that was supposed to be from the 1800's the wood was smooth like it had been sanded, which made the dresser a lot less valuable. The grooves in another dresser were perfectly lined up, something that was impossible with the tools available in the 19th century.

"I think we should go back to the store and demand our money back," Tyler said.

"You're absolutely right," Aunt Michele said. "I feel like I have been robbed again."

Luckily, they had only unloaded a couple pieces of furniture and after loading them back on the truck they said good-bye to Bobbie.

Because everyone could not fit into the borrowed truck, Aunt Michele drove her car and followed Tyler. It was almost an hour's drive to the antique store so Tyler, Steve, and Michael had plenty of time to play car games, and even sing along while Stephanie rode with her aunt. As they drove into Boulder, the kids were finishing the alphabet game.

"Y is for yellow," Michael said, pointing to a yellow caution sign.

"Z - zoo" Steve said for the last letter in the game.

"I don't see any zoo," Michael said.

"The Denver Zoo is in that direction, you just can't see it," Steve answered jokingly.

But when they arrived at the antique store they found it locked, and it was no laughing matter. The sign in the window still said open and the hours on the sign read open until 5 o'clock that day but it was only a little after 3 o'clock.

"Maybe they just went out to get a sandwich," Aunt Michele said.

"But when we were here a few hours ago there were two people working, so just one of them could have left," Tyler said.

"I bet they knew that we would be back so they just closed up," Stephanie said.

"Well, closing the store isn't going to stop us," Aunt Michele said. "We'll be back, but for now let's go get some ice cream."

They walked across the street to the ice cream parlor. No one said anything along the way and not much was said as they ate their ice cream. They had a clear view of the antique store from the booth that they sat in.

"I haven't seen anyone go in or out of the store," Stephanie said.

"Someone could have gone out the back door," her twin brother, Steve, said.

"Don't worry kids we'll catch up with those crooks sooner or later," Aunt Michele said.

But after they finished their ice cream, they found the store still closed and no one was in sight. They were leaving when Steve noticed that one thing about the store had changed. The sign in the window that had said open earlier now said closed. He pointed it out to the others.

"I bet they have been here all along," he said.

For several minutes they took turns pounding on the door to the antique store but, as they had already assumed, no one answered.

"We're not giving up that easily," Tyler said.

"They can't keep it closed forever," Steve commented.

"You boys are right, but I think right now we are wasting our time," Aunt Michele said.

"What do you think we should do now?" Stephanie asked her aunt.

"I saw several garage sale signs coming into town," she said.

"Maybe some of them have antiques for sale," Michael said, immediately picking up on his mom's train of thought.

"Exactly," his mother said, smiling.

"What are we waiting for?" Stephanie, who enjoyed garage sales, said.

"Do you think it's all right to leave Brian's truck parked here?" Tyler asked his aunt.

"That sounds like a good idea," Aunt Michele agreed. "We won't be gone very long."

"And then we can check on the store again when we get back," Steve pointed out.

But when the family returned a few hours later, they found the store just as they had left it. On the bright side, going to several garage sales had turned out to be worthwhile. Aunt Michele bought some antique toys, a few old books, and a set of dishes. She also bought an old dresser and a matching chest of drawers. The only problem was that since Aunt Michele had driven up in her car, they had no way of carrying it back with them. The sellers agreed to hold the furniture for them to pick up the next morning.

"It's too bad that there isn't room on the truck to carry the furniture back," Steve said.

"We would have had plenty of room if we had been able to unload this junk," Tyler said.

"And I really would like to return Brian's truck," Aunt Michele said frowning. "I think that if we can't return the furniture tomorrow when we come up, we should just unload the furniture and return the truck."

"Can you sell the reproductions?" Stephanie asked her aunt.

"I am sure that I can but I won't make a profit," Aunt Michele replied.

Everyone went to bed early that night. The following day was Saturday and Aunt Michele wanted to go to some more garage sales. After breakfast Tyler suggested unloading the truck for the time being so that they could haul any furniture that they might find.

After Aunt Michele tried phoning Sandra's Antiques and got no answer, she agreed that unloading the reproductions was probably a good idea. As Tyler and Steve started to unload the furniture, a neighbor of Aunt Michele's noticed and came over to help. With the three of them working together it still took an hour to move all of the furniture into Aunt Michele's house.

"A lot of work for nothing," Aunt Michele said frowning.

"Cheer up, we've got some garage sales to go to," Stephanie reminded her aunt.

While the boys moved furniture the two of them looked through the newspaper for garage sale ads. They had marked several that advertised selling furniture and they had even mapped some so they could hit the closest while it was still early. Aunt Michele's mood changed as she pulled up to the first garage sale and saw several pieces of furniture sitting out in front.

"I think we better get our muscles ready," Tyler told his brother as they pulled up behind.

"It looks like Aunt Michele is already bargaining," Steve agreed as they got out of the truck.

Aunt Michele had spotted an old china cabinet that was probably from the late thirties. She knew that the cabinet probably wasn't much newer than that because it was made with real glass instead of Plexiglass, which was used widely after being invented in 1931.

"How much do you want for this china cabinet?" she asked as her nephews joined her.

After the price was quoted Aunt Michele immediately said she would take it without hesitation. As Tyler and Steve carefully loaded the cabinet using a handcart, Aunt Michele also bought a set of lamps, some candles, and an old coffee table.

"Let's head back to the garage sale from yesterday," Aunt Michele said after paying for the items. "I want to pick up the dresser and chest of drawers that they are holding for me."

"Sounds like a good idea, the house isn't very far from here," Tyler agreed.

Reaching the house they saw that the garage sale was still going on. The owners were happy to see them.

"We've had a lot of people ask us about the furniture," they said. "Thank you for picking up the items."

"No, thank you for holding the furniture for me," Aunt Michele said.

"I'm glad that they kept their word," Steve said as he got in the truck.

"Yeah, I was a little nervous about them holding the furniture after what has happened," Tyler said. "It's nice to know that most people are good."

The next few garage sales were a disappointment, with mainly baby items and modern pieces of furniture for sale. Before heading to the next sale, Aunt Michele decided to call Sandra's Antiques but again there was no answer.

"Cheer up, Aunt Michele, we have more garage sales on our list," Stephanie reminded her aunt.

"You're right," Aunt Michele said.

Arriving at the next sale, their aunt soon saw that she definitely had something to smile about. Tyler soon saw the item also as he pulled in behind his aunt's car. He gasped and started to turn the truck around so he could back it up to the drive.

"What's wrong?" Steve asked his brother in confusion.

"Look what I see," Tyler said.

Aunt Michele had already started paying for the item and had motioned to Tyler to load it.

"What is that?" Steve asked, not recognizing the item that Aunt Michele was standing next to.

"It's an old ice box from the nineteenth century used to keep food cold before there were refrigerators," Tyler told his brother.

"Wow, what a find at a garage sale," Steve exclaimed.

After loading the ice box onto the truck, Aunt Michele asked Tyler to park the truck next to the drive. When he was done, she explained that the girl's grandmother had recently passed away and a truck full of her belongings would soon be arriving. The family waited several minutes while the granddaughter apologized for the wait.

"My brother should be here anytime," she said.

"We really don't mind waiting," Aunt Michele said and then added, "but I think I'll try to call Sandra's Antiques once more."

After making the call the teenagers could tell by the look on her face that she hadn't gotten an answer. A few minutes later a pickup truck full off antiques pulled up.

Aunt Michele bought almost everything on the truck, including an old phonograph, an antique washing machine, and an old sewing machine. She also bought some wash boards and some old seventy-two records. The teenagers, with the help of the girl's brother and his friend, loaded the items directly from one truck to the other.

When they were done, Steve inquired about lunch.

"I just want to make one more stop before lunch," Aunt Michele said.

Arriving at the next garage sale, the teenagers thought that they had found another antique, an old desk, but they soon learned that it really wasn't that old.

"Oh, well," Aunt Michele said. "I can't complain. I have never found so many antiques at garage sales in one day."

"I couldn't believe it when I saw that old ice box," Tyler told his aunt later.

"You should have heard Aunt Michele in the car, she was so excited," Stephanie told them.

Aunt Michele just grinned and changed the subject. "So where do you kids want to eat?"

"Somewhere I can get a big hoagie," Steve replied.

"How about going to a restaurant along Pearl Street Mall?" Stephanie suggested.

"That's a great idea," Aunt Michele quickly agreed. "Maybe I can find a gift for your parent's anniversary."

"Mom and Dad's anniversary!" Tyler exclaimed.

"We forgot all about it," Stephanie said. "We better start thinking about it."

When the family reached Pearl Street Mall, they found the outdoor shops bustling with excitement. Outside the many shops, an art festival was taking place, with hundreds of artists displaying their artwork.

"Maybe I could get Mom and Dad a painting," Stephanie said, looking over the artwork. But she soon found most of the paintings were out of her price range.

"Before we go shopping, can we get some grub?" Steve asked. "There's a sandwich shop over on that corner."

"Sounds good to me," Tyler said. "Can you order me a turkey on rye with mustard, pickle, and onion?"

"Sure, where are you going?" Steve asked his brother.

"Just over there," Tyler pointed to a man who appeared to be drawing caricatures.

When Tyler returned to the sandwich shop he asked his brother and sister to sit with him after lunch for a caricature drawing.

"I think that's a silly gift," Stephanie said.

"Yeah, so, I like it," Tyler answered.

Aunt Michele thought it was a great idea and, after the picture was done, even Stephanie liked it.

They were walking around looking at the different types of artwork when they came to a wood carver. As Stephanie was looking at the unique pictures that the man had carved out, Steve and Tyler were eyeing a tall, wooden eagle.

"Mom and Dad would love this," Steve said.

"Yeah, maybe we should have pooled our money," Tyler agreed.

Stephanie picked out a carved picture of an elk in front of a mountain with a mirrored lake.

"Okay, I'm ready," she said.

"I have to pay for this first," Aunt Michele said, standing next to the eagle.

"What?" Tyler and Steve said together.

"I haven't bought your parents an anniversary gift yet, either," she said.

"They will love..." Stephanie started to say but Tyler interrupted the rest of her comment.

"Look, I think it's Mr. Gomez!" he said, pointing to a man with dark hair.

"Mr. Gomez, is that you?" Tyler called to the man.

The dark-haired man stopped and looked behind him toward the teenagers and then, as if he had recognized them, he took off. Before Aunt Michele had a chance to say anything, the teenagers were chasing him.

"Wait, we won't be able to find each other!" Aunt Michele called through the crowd of people.

"Meet us at the car," Tyler called back.

Michael couldn't run as fast as his cousins so he decided to stay behind with his mother. It wasn't until several minutes later that the teenagers met them at the car.

"Did you catch up to him?" she asked.

"Oh, we caught him all right," Stephanie said.

"That's great," Aunt Michele said. "But why don't you sound too happy about it?"

"We lost the man that looked like Mr. Gomez and started chasing a man with a red cap," Tyler said. "Finally, the guy turned around and we knew right away that it wasn't him."

"Well, don't worry about it," Aunt Michele said. "They can't keep the store closed forever."

Everyone agreed but the next day when they visited Sandra's Antiques once more, their hopes were dashed. Tyler was the first to walk up to the front door.

"Oh, no!" he exclaimed.

When the others asked him what was wrong, he told them to look in the window.

"It's empty," the twins said, almost in unison.

"I can't believe this," Aunt Michele said, furiously. "They made a run for it!"

Chapter 3
Interesting Find

The door to Sandra's Antique store opened easily when Tyler reached for it. The family cautiously walked in the building, calling "Hello?" to anyone who might have been inside but no one replied. The room was completely empty with only dust balls on the floor.

"They sure hit the road fast," Tyler said, as he looked around the room.

"Now what do we do?" Stephanie asked.

"I think that we better call the police and file a report," Aunt Michele replied.

The clerk at the police department said that it would be at least half an hour until she could send an officer out to file a report. They decided to use the time to go into the stores around the antique shop to inquire into the store owner's whereabouts. But none of the other store owners had an answer for them; they were just as surprised as the Thompson family.

"They were open just a couple of days ago," one of the managers said. "It's like they vanished in the middle of the night."

Just as they were leaving the last store, they saw a patrol car pull up. They explained the situation to Officer

Harris, who was very nice. Unfortunately, the officer informed them that their best bet was to talk to a lawyer.

"If you can locate these people, maybe you'll have some legal options," Officer Harris said.

"Well, we're not any better off now that we talked to the police department," Aunt Michele said after the officer had left.

"Don't worry, we'll figure something out," Tyler said.

The family left the store discouraged that they didn't have any leads as to where the owners might be. As they were getting in the car, Aunt Michele pulled a business card out of her purse.

"I almost forgot, I picked up this business card the last time I was at the antique store," she said. "The names on the card are Hernandez and Anita Gomez. We will look them up in the phone book and give them a surprise home visit."

But unfortunately their address wasn't in the phone book and after calling the operator they found out that their phone number was unlisted.

The next stop on their itinerary was an estate sale in Lyons. Tyler had driven Brian's truck again in hopes of finding more antiques.

"I hope we can get some good deals," Aunt Michele said, as they pulled into the driveway of a farm in the country. The sale was being held in a big red barn in back of the house. "I only saw this sale advertised in one paper so hopefully I won't have a lot of dealers to compete with."

Despite the fact that there were a lot of dealers that somehow had heard about the sale, Aunt Michele managed to get what she thought were some really good deals. Aunt Michele bought an oak secretary's desk dating back to the 1800's, a heavy rocker designed in the roaring twenties, and a primitive shaker table.

"It's a good thing that we waited to return this truck," Tyler said, as he and his brother loaded the items. "It would have been a tight fit to put all three pieces on Dad's truck."

The family headed back to Aunt Michele's, where they unloaded the antiques so they could return the borrowed truck. Not much was said as they moved the furniture into their aunt's house. When they were done, they ordered some Chinese food, which Tyler and Aunt Michele went to pick up after returning the borrowed truck.

That night the family played a board game together.

"This is fun," Michael said.

"We are really going to miss you kids when you leave," Aunt Michele said.

"You're not getting rid of us anytime soon," Tyler said. "We want to be here for your opening day."

"Opening day isn't that far away, it's this Saturday," Aunt Michele told them.

"This Saturday!" Steve exclaimed. "Do you think we have enough furniture?"

"I think that I have a good inventory to start with and hopefully, we can find some additional pieces over the next couple of days," Aunt Michele said.

The next morning when the teenagers awoke, they found their aunt fixing breakfast.

"It will soon be my opening day, and I am going to be busy," she said. "In the meantime, I thought we could do something fun."

"What are we going to do?" Steve asked.

"I thought we could walk around downtown Fort Collins," Aunt Michele told them.

"That sounds like fun," Stephanie said.

"I still have to get Mom and Dad an anniversary gift," Steve said.

Fort Collins was a college town, and there were lots of sidewalk cafes, and unique gift shops in the downtown area. They saw a lot of young artists trying to sell their work and musicians hoping to make a few extra dollars. Steve decided on a pocketknife for his father and a necklace for his mother. After paying for the gifts, the family headed back to Aunt Michele's house.

That night, Aunt Michele was looking for boxes and wrapping paper for their anniversary gifts when the phone rang.

"It's for you, Tyler" she said. "It's Officer Harris." She handed Tyler the phone.

"Yes, that's right; the name was Sandra's Antiques, why do you ask?" Tyler asked the officer.

"We just got a bulletin about that place. Can you describe the salespeople that helped you?" he answered.

After Tyler had described the salespeople, the officer said that his description matched the one on the bulletin.

"I hate to tell you this, but you got off easier than a lot of people," the officer said. "Those people closed up and took with them the furniture that people had on layaway and some that was supposed to be delivered."

After Tyler hung up the phone, he filled everyone in on their conversation.

"It seems we are not the only ones that these people ripped off; they got away with a lot of furniture and money," he said. "Officer Harris wants us to keep in contact with him, and let him know if we find these people."

The following morning they had a trip to Fort Morgan, Colorado, planned so they could attend another sale that Aunt Michele had read about in the paper.

"It didn't say anything about having antiques, just furniture," she told them. "But a lot of times people have antiques and don't know it."

Unfortunately, that wasn't the case this time. The closest thing to an antique that was for sale was a manual typewriter. Even though there were no antiques, none of them went home empty handed. The boys bought some fishing tackle, Stephanie bought some new CD's, and Aunt Michele got a good deal on some books about archeology, a hobby of hers.

After stopping for lunch, the family headed back to Aunt Michele's, where there still was plenty of work for them to do.

"We still have to rearrange the furniture," Aunt Michele said.

As they looked around the room, the new wallpaper looked nice but the furniture was scattered around in bunches. The teenagers immediately started to move the furniture without Aunt Michele saying another word.

"The dressers and taller furniture should go along this back wall," Tyler said as he tied a dresser to a hand-cart so he could move it.

After the taller furniture was moved to the back wall, the desks were placed along the side wall, and the tables moved to the center of the room. As Steve and Tyler moved the bigger furniture, Aunt Michele and Stephanie moved the smaller pieces. Soon the room was starting to look like a store.

"Now, we just have to hang the pictures," Aunt Michele said as she stepped back to admire the room.

As the brothers hung the pictures, Stephanie washed the windows.

"The store looks perfect," Aunt Michele said when they were done. "Let's get some dinner so we can get to bed, tomorrow is a big day."

Opening day of Mayfair Antiques was an exciting day for everyone. The teenagers had put up flyers around town and a banner across the entrance announcing the grand opening. Coffee, juice and pastry were served to the customers. The first sale wasn't for three hours after opening, but Aunt Michele received several compliments on her selection of furniture. She even managed to sell a reproduction at the same price she had paid for it to a lady who was looking for a desk, not necessarily an antique. Tyler and Steve carried the desk out to the woman's car.

"That's strange," Steve said under his breath but loud enough for Tyler to hear.

"What's that?" Tyler asked.

"Well, maybe it's my imagination but it looks like some kind of word was written on the bottom of this desk," Steve said.

As Tyler looked closer to where Steve was looking he could read the word "Madison" very faintly.

"It looks like it says "Madison," but it isn't easy to make out," Tyler said. "The word could be the key to where the desk came from in the first place.

Steve agreed with his brother as they finished loading it in the woman's car.

"Let's check the other pieces of furniture and see if they are marked also," Tyler said.

Together the boys started looking at the bottom of each piece of furniture. All of the reproductions were the same with "Madison" carved on the bottom, some were fainter than others but could still be read if you looked close enough.

"Didn't Aunt Michele say that she had bought that antique desk that's in her office from the same company a few years ago?" Tyler asked his brother.

"That's right, she did," Steve answered.

Steve understood exactly what his brother was getting at. They knew that the desk was supposed to be authentic and therefore should not be marked on the bottom. After examining the bottom of the desk, the boys were able to prove this theory.

"Officer Harris should hear about this clue," Tyler said picking up the phone.

"It doesn't seem like much now, but it could really mean something later in this case," the officer said. "I would like to come down to the store so you can show me what you're talking about."

It was early afternoon when the officer walked in the door of Mayfair Antiques. Aunt Michele was surprised to see him since she didn't know about the phone call that Tyler had made.

"Is anything wrong?" she asked.

"I phoned Officer Harris about a clue we found," Tyler said, stepping in.

Tyler showed them the carved marking that they had discovered on the desk.

"That is very interesting," Aunt Michele said.

"By the way, I have some news for you," Officer Harris said. "The Gomez's are not the owners of Sandra's Antiques. The real owner is Sandra McGlothan, who has been vacationing in Arizona," he said.

"Is she aware of what the Gomez's have been doing?" Aunt Michele asked.

"She is now, and is on her way back," the officer told them. "She sounded really upset when I explained that they cleaned her entire store out. Hopefully, she can give us a clue about where to look for Hernandez and Anita Gomez."

The officer thanked Tyler again for calling him and said it could be a big lead in their investigation.

Later that night the family was seated around the television set watching a science fiction movie when their Aunt Marybeth showed up. After all of the family hugs, she explained that she had been driving through the area with her friend, Nitza. They had stopped at an antique store and Aunt Marybeth had found a good deal on an antique desk.

"When I saw the desk, I immediately thought of you, Sis," she explained. "You can consider it a birthday gift."

"We want you to have a great opening," Nitza added.

"Thanks, that's awful nice of you," Aunt Michele said.

Unfortunately, Aunt Michele had not yet noticed the one flaw with the piece of furniture. Underneath on the bottom of the desk, Tyler showed Steve and Stephanie the word "Madison" that stood out like a sore thumb.

Chapter 4
Another Puzzle Piece

"Aunt Marybeth, where did you say that you bought the desk?" Tyler asked.

"We went to a conference in Cheyenne and there was a tiny antique shop not too far from where we were staying," Aunt Marybeth answered.

"Do you remember the name of the store?" Stephanie asked her aunt.

"I have a business card here somewhere," she answered as she looked in her purse. "Here it is. It was called Red Barn Antiques."

She handed Aunt Michele the card, "in case you want to take a drive, they seemed to have some great deals."

"Of course, they have some great deals," Tyler thought to himself. "It was easy to sell fake copies of antiques cheap and still make a hefty profit."

As the movie ended the teenagers left their aunts so that they could visit. They didn't say a word about the mark that they saw on the bottom of the desk. They knew if the piece of furniture was a fake, Aunt Michele had more than likely already figured that out, whether she had seen the name "Madison" yet or not. Aunt Michele was too polite to say anything. Once they were upstairs and out of earshot, the teenagers discussed the word "Madison" that was imprinted on the desk.

"We have to do some research on the word imprinted on these reproductions," Tyler said as he turned on his laptop computer. "Maybe we will find a Madison Company on the Internet."

But after using several different search engines, Tyler couldn't find a furniture company named Madison anywhere on the Web.

"Maybe the word just refers to Madison, Wisconsin," Steve pointed out.

Tyler and Stephanie looked at each other knowing their brother was right. They had just decided that the best place to start their research would be at the library when the phone rang. After Aunt Michele had hung up the phone, she called to the others.

"Tomorrow night we are going out to dinner to celebrate," she said.

"What's the occasion?" Stephanie asked.

"That was Sandra McGlothan, owner of Sandra's Antiques, on the phone," Aunt Michele said. "She feels real bad about what her managers did, and said to bring the furniture by the store tomorrow and she would write me a refund check."

The next morning the teenagers volunteered to return the furniture and pick up the check so that Aunt Michele could watch the store. When they arrived at the store, they found it much different than their first couple of visits. The sign in the window still said closed but the doors and windows were wide open. A friendly lady who was busy sweeping the floors greeted them. She introduced herself as Sandra and asked them how she could be of help. When Tyler told her who they were, she apologized again for all their trouble. She said that she couldn't believe that her managers, who had come highly recommended, would do such a thing.

"Where do you want the furniture?" Tyler asked, as he unloaded the reproductions.

"You can just set them in this corner," Sandra replied. "I am hoping to sell them to someone who deals with reproductions."

After all of the furniture had been moved, Sandra handed Tyler a check.

"Do you have any idea where the Gomez's might be?" Tyler asked.

"I only wish I knew! I've tried going to their home but either no one has been home or they're just not answering the door," she said.

"Could you give us the address?" Tyler asked. "We would like to try again."

As Sandra was writing down the address for them, Stephanie asked if she knew any relatives of the Gomez's.

"I know they had family somewhere near Cheyenne," Sandra said. "The police have a warrant out for their arrest, and they are searching the area."

"What do you know about the word "Madison" being imprinted on the reproductions?" Tyler asked the woman.

"What do you mean?" Sandra asked.

Tyler started to show her what he meant when she suddenly gasped.

"I don't recognize this furniture at all," she said. "I would sure like to know where they got this furniture."

After thanking Sandra for being so nice, Tyler headed north to the town of Fort Lupton to the address she had given them. The Gomez's lived on a small farm outside of town. There were no cars parked in front of the small house, just a couple of goats wandering around eating the grass. In the field next to the house, cows were grazing on the land. They knocked on the door but no one answered.

"It doesn't look like anyone is home," Tyler said.

"Now what do we do?" Stephanie asked.

"How about getting some lunch," Steve suggested.

"Lunch?" Stephanie questioned, laughing. "It wasn't that long ago that we ate breakfast."

"Can I help it if I have an active metabolism?" Steve asked.

"So where do you want to eat?" Tyler asked, knowing it was best just to give in to his brother.

"There's a sandwich shop on that corner over there," Steve said.

"You sure have a keen eye for food," Stephanie said teasingly.

At the sandwich shop, Steve ordered a large cheesesteak sandwich, Tyler got a small ham and cheese, and

Stephanie ordered a salad. While they were waiting for their food, Stephanie decided to check the phone booth to look up the name, Gomez.

"Maybe they are visiting some relatives," she said. But when she returned she had bad news. "There are two long columns of Gomez's in the phone book."

"Did you check for a Madison company?" Tyler asked.

"No. That's a good idea," Stephanie said as the waitress served their food.

After the teenagers finished eating they checked the phone book but didn't find any Madison company listed.

"Why don't we stop by the library?" Tyler suggested when he spotted it.

At the library, they soon learned that there weren't any businesses in Colorado registered as the Madison Company. They decided to check the states bordering Colorado and soon found a Madison Company in Cheyenne, Wyoming. Unfortunately, the only information listed about the company was its address.

"At least it's a start," Stephanie said as she copied the information.

"What does the company manufacture?" Tyler asked his brother, who cross-referenced the name under the list of manufacturers.

"The name isn't here," Steve said after double-checking the index.

"Well, we are not very far from Cheyenne; maybe we can take a drive up there," Tyler said. "Right now let's get this check back to Aunt Michele."

Aunt Michele was very excited to see the teenagers when they arrived back at her house.

"I am getting this check right to the bank," she said. "Can you watch the store for me?"

"Sure, no problem," Tyler told his aunt.

When Aunt Michele returned she asked the kids where they would like to go for dinner.

"Why don't we try that new Mexican restaurant down the street?" Michael said.

For once the teenagers all agreed that Mexican food sounded good and after ordering Aunt Michele told them about the church picnic the following afternoon.

"I've been so busy that I forgot to tell you kids all about the picnic our church is having after worship services tomorrow," she said.

"It sounds like fun," Stephanie said.

"Yeah, is it too late to get in on the softball game?" Tyler asked.

"I'm sure you kids can play," Aunt Michele replied.

After services the next day, the Thompson family gathered around with several other families on the front lawn of the church. There was plenty of food and games to play, including a softball tournament with the adult and teen Sunday school classes.

Before helping themselves to the food, the teenagers picked the games that they wanted to take part in. All of them wanted to play in the softball tournament except for Stephanie, who wanted to play volleyball.

"I'll join you in the volleyball game," Aunt Michele said. "It's more my speed."

"Cool," Stephanie said.

"Of course, we'll be on opposite sides since it's the adults against the teenagers," Aunt Michele said.

Just then Aunt Michele's friend, Nicole, and her daughter, Caitlyn joined them.

"What games are you playing in?" she asked.

"The boys are playing softball but my niece, Stephanie, and I are playing volleyball," Aunt Michele told her.

"Mom and I are also playing volleyball," Caitlyn said.

"Is Brandon playing softball?" Aunt Michele asked, noticing that Nicole's oldest son was standing with the softball team.

"Yeah, he is going to pitch for the youth group," Nicole replied.

"My older brother, Tyler, is a good pitcher," Stephanie told Nicole.

"Maybe they will have him pitch after a few innings," Nicole said.

The foursome watched as the softball game started before the volleyball game. The game was already in the third inning and the adults were ahead by two runs by the time the volleyball game started.

"So I hear you are helping your aunt get her store open," Caitlyn said to Stephanie as they joined the other teenagers to play volleyball against the adults.

"We are trying to help her replace her inventory but it hasn't been easy," Stephanie replied and went on to explain about the store managers that had skipped town after tricking them.

"That's terrible," Caitlyn said after Stephanie was done.

"It gets better; the owner didn't know what was going on and refunded the money that my aunt paid," Stephanie said. Then she added, "What's terrible is how we are letting the adults win this game!"

Just then Caitlyn missed the volleyball as it was passed right to her causing their side to go out.

"I'm not much help," she said frowning at her mistake.

"You just need to concentrate," Stephanie told her new friend. "I'm sure our conversation isn't helping so I'll tell you the rest of the story after the game."

Caitlyn quickly agreed that was a good idea as their team took possession of the ball and it was now her turn to serve. At first it didn't look like her serve was going to make it over the net but it just barely did. In the end, the teenagers lost the match as they only won one out of three games.

In the meantime, the teenagers on the softball tournament were now winning the game. Tyler was now pitching for the youth group. As the volleyball game ended, the softball game was at the bottom of the last inning. Tyler pitched three strikes to the last batter to win the game.

After the game everyone was served homemade ice cream. While the boys talked mainly about the softball game, Stephanie and Caitlyn had a chance to finish their conversation about Aunt Michele's business.

"I am glad things are working out for you," Caitlyn told Aunt Michele as they were leaving. "I love looking at antiques and I can't wait to come by."

"That would be nice," Aunt Michele said, smiling.

The next morning after breakfast, the teenagers headed up to Cheyenne. Before reaching the city, Tyler stopped at a gas station and bought a map.

"It looks like the company is located downtown in the historical district," he said after finding the street on the map.

They continued to the historical section of town where they found many abandoned buildings. Soon Steve spotted an older building that had the "Madison Company" sign on the side of it.

"It's over there," Steve said, pointing it out.

Tyler pulled in front of the building that Steve had spotted and parked the car.

"It looks abandoned," Stephanie said.

"It could be but it's hard to tell," Tyler commented. "Let's go investigate."

The building was an old warehouse with steps leading to the entrance. The teen detectives climbed to the top where they found the door to the building locked. They hesitated for a moment trying to plan their next move. If they knocked and someone answered, what would they say? Tyler decided to ask for directions if anyone answered, and then he knocked loudly.

"No one is in there," he said after several moments.

"We are no better off than before," Stephanie said.

"If only we could get a look inside," Tyler said.

"There is a window up there," Steve said, pointing.

"I saw that," Tyler said nodding. "It's worth a try."

"Wait a minute guys," Stephanie said, understanding their idea. "That fire escape may not be sturdy enough; this looks like a really old building."

"Don't worry, I'll be careful," Tyler said.

"And what if something happens, who is going to go for help?" Stephanie said.

"Stephanie is right, better let me climb up," Steve said.

"Okay, but if it feels loose, you're to climb right back down," Tyler said as he helped his younger brother up to the first step.

Steve slowly ascended the old stairs up to the window. The rungs were a little wobbly but seemed stable. When he had reached the top, he peeked in the window. After a few minutes of looking in the window, Steve climbed back down as carefully as he had climbed up.

"Did you see anything?" Tyler asked once he was down.

"All I could see was an empty room," Steve replied.

"I guess this is just a dead end," Tyler started to say when they heard someone unlocking the front door.

The door opened suddenly and a tall man with a dark complexion appeared before them.

"What do you kids want?" he grumbled.

"We got lost and wanted directions," Tyler said quickly.

"Directions huh, get off my property before I call the police!" the man said as he went back inside the building and slammed and dead-bolted the door.

Chapter 5
Disaster

"What a grump!" Stephanie said. "I'll bet he has something to hide."

"Maybe he saw Steve climbing the fire escape and knew that our story wasn't true," Tyler said.

"Even so, he was still rude," Steve said. "I wonder who he is?"

"Maybe he's the owner," Michael said.

"That's a possibility," Stephanie said. "Or he could be homeless."

"Or a criminal who's hiding out," Tyler added. "We better get out of here while we still can."

Steve and Stephanie headed for the car, quickly agreeing with their brother.

"We'll try to do some more research on the Madison Company over the Internet now that we know that there is a company by that name in Cheyenne," Tyler said as he drove back to Aunt Michele's.

They found their aunt happily humming away in her antique store when they returned. Apparently she'd had a good morning and had made several sales.

"Are you kids ready for lunch?" she asked. "I thought I would make some macaroni and cheese."

"That sounds good, but I can make it so you don't have to leave the store," Stephanie volunteered.

"All right, I'm sure you can handle it," Aunt Michele quickly agreed.

While Stephanie was making lunch the boys were researching the name "Madison" over the Internet. Tyler decided to start at the Cheyenne tourist site.

"Here it is," he said excitedly. "It is under a list of manufacturers in Cheyenne."

Tyler read more about the company to learn that they made antique reproductions, and the owner of the company was a man named Tom Dunn.

"I wonder if that's the man who told us to leave?" he commented.

"The listing gives the company's phone number," Steve said. "We could give Mr. Dunn a call and ask him some questions."

"Yeah, maybe we can tell by the sound of his voice if he is the same man that we saw," Michael said.

"That's not a bad idea, but what can we ask him?" Tyler questioned.

"We'll ask him straight out how he thinks he'll get away with selling his reproductions as actual antiques," Steve said.

After disconnecting from the internet, Tyler turned on the speakerphone so that they could all listen and dialed the phone number listed. When a man answered, he asked for Tom Dunn.

"This is Tom Dunn speaking; what can I do for you?" the man replied.

"Mr. Dunn, I am not going to beat around the bush," Tyler said, trying to disguise his voice to sound older. "Do you really think you can get away with what you're trying to do?"

"What on earth are you talking about?" the man replied loudly.

"It is a well-known fact that your company manufactures reproductions, yet you are trying to sell the pieces of furniture as actual antiques," Tyler said.

"I am doing nothing of the sort. Look, I don't know who you think you are but you can't go around making accusations about hard-working citizens," Mr. Dunn said as he slammed down the phone.

"That call certainly didn't get us anywhere," Tyler said after he had hung up the phone.

"Maybe he's telling the truth," Steve said.

"Yeah, maybe it's Mr. Gomez who's trying to pass the furniture off as actual antiques," Michael said.

"That certainly is possible," Tyler agreed. "We should be investigating Hernandez and Anita Gomez."

"If the Gomez's are innocent, then why would they disappear," Michael said.

"That's a good point," Steve agreed.

"Lunch is ready," Stephanie said, joining them. "What are you guys talking about?"

The boys took turns explaining about their phone call to the Madison Company and talking to Mr. Dunn.

"Do you think it was the same man that we saw?" Stephanie asked.

"It's hard to tell with such a short conversation," Tyler said. "His voice did sound similar."

After lunch the teenagers decided to go see a new movie that had just come out. All of them enjoyed the movie and were still commenting on it during the drive back to Aunt Michele's.

"Those sound effects were awesome," Steve said.

"Yeah, the sounds of the explosions were really cool," Michael said.

"I thought the movie was very realistic," Stephanie said. "I really liked it."

Back at Mayfair Antiques, the teenagers found their aunt busy dusting off all of the antiques.

"Not one person has been in since you kids left," she said. "But I've been busy so the time went by fast. I even made dinner which should be almost ready."

After dinner the teenagers were playing a board game when Aunt Michele suggested that they go out for some ice cream.

"That is, if you kids are not too full," she said.

"I'm never too full for ice cream," Stephanie said.

"Yeah, I think I can find some room as long as it's chocolate," Steve said.

"I'm making mine butterscotch," Tyler said.

"Mm, that sounds good too," Steve said thoughtfully.

By the time that they got to the ice cream shop they had each changed the flavor of ice cream that they wanted several times. All of them, that is, except for Aunt Michele, who decided on her favorite ice cream flavor, strawberry.

The next morning, Aunt Michele informed the teenagers that there was an estate sale in Broomfield, a suburb of Denver that she planned on attending that day.

"Steve and I can watch the store again," Stephanie immediately volunteered.

"Oh no, this time you have to come with us," she said. "My friend, Bobbie, is going to watch the store while we are gone."

"Are you sure, because we really don't mind?" Stephanie started to say.

"I insist that you come along, besides we might do something fun afterwards," Aunt Michele said.

"Like what?" Michael asked immediately.

"You'll see, it's a surprise," Aunt Michele said smiling.

Aunt Michele made bids on several items at the estate sale but all except one of the items, an old schoolhouse clock, went for more money than she wanted to pay. After the sale the family headed south toward the city of Denver.

It was soon easy to figure out where they were going. All three teenagers cheered as they parked across from Coors Field. It had been awhile since they had attended a Rockies baseball game and it sounded like fun.

"I promised you kids a baseball game," she said.

"That's right. I forgot all about that," Michael told his mother.

"Dad is going to be so jealous," Tyler said. "He loves baseball and his favorite team is the Colorado Rockies."

"I hope that they win," Stephanie said. "They lost the last game that we went to."

"They are on a winning streak right now," Steve, whose favorite sport was baseball, informed them. "They have won four out of the last five games."

After they bought their tickets for the game, they went straight to the concession stand where they loaded up on hot dogs, soda, and peanuts. Then they found their seats, which were right above the bullpen, where they could watch the pitcher warming up.

Soon the game against the Los Angeles Dodgers was underway, with the Dodgers up to bat. The Rockies managed to get three outs quickly without any runs scored. During their turn at bat they got three hits and brought in two runs, giving the Rockies the lead from the beginning. The rest of the game turned out to be really tight. At the top of the ninth, the Dodgers and the Rockies were tied at three runs each, and the Dodgers had two men on base with the Dodgers' star hitter up to bat and there was only one out.

"Strike one," the umpire called.

"That's one," Steve said as he held his breath for the next pitch.

Again the hitter got a strike.

"Only one more," Stephanie said.

But on the next pitch the batter made contact and hit a single into right field. The right fielder threw the ball to the catcher and the runner from second couldn't score, so now the bases were loaded. The next hitter quickly got in a hole with two strikes and no balls when he hit a line drive to the shortstop. He immediately stepped on second base for a double play, and the third out. Everyone was on their feet cheering and yelling.

"Yes, a double play!" Steve exclaimed.

Now it was the Rockies' turn up, and they were on fire. They got two runs on a home run by their first baseman and won the game.

"That was such a close game," Aunt Michele said. "I thought the game was over with three men on base and only one out in the ninth."

"I had faith," Steve smiled.

"Me, too," Tyler said.

"Me, three," Stephanie laughed.

The next day, the teenagers decided to drive back down to the Gomez's farm one more time. This time it looked much different from when they had first visited. There were several kids playing in the front yard. A woman was also outside hanging clothes on a clothesline.

"¿en qué puedo servirle?" she asked.

Luckily, Tyler understood a little Spanish and knew that she had asked if she could help them.

"We are looking for the Gomez's" Tyler said.

"Gomez?" the woman answered. "They are not here."

"Do you know where they went?" Stephanie asked but the woman didn't understand.

The woman yelled in Spanish to one of her children. Soon a boy, who looked to be about sixteen, ran over to her.

"We are looking for Hernandez and Anita Gomez," Tyler told the boy.

"They are gone," the boy answered for his mother. "Sold us farm cheap, and left."

"Do you have any idea where they went?" Stephanie asked again.

"No, they were in a big hurry," he answered.

"The Gomez's are wanted by the police," Tyler told the boy.

"The police?" the boy said surprised.

"The police, the police!" Suddenly the older woman was frantic. It was obvious that she understood the word, police.

Tyler immediately told the boy to explain to the woman not to worry, that they were not in trouble. Then, he asked the boy to call Officer Harris if he saw the Gomez family again.

Back at Aunt Michele's house, the teenagers found their aunt setting the table.

"You're just in time, I am taking dinner out of the oven," she told them. "Go wash up."

As they sat down to dinner, Aunt Michele turned the television on to the evening news where a breaking news story was underway. Apparently, one of the old warehouses in a historical district of Cheyenne was on fire.

"Look!" Tyler said, recognizing the building.

"It's the Madison Company," Steve exclaimed.

Chapter 6
Recognized

As the Thompson kids and their aunt watched the news bulletin, they soon learned that the fire was under investigation.

"I bet they set the fire on purpose, probably to destroy some kind of evidence or possibly for the insurance money," Tyler said.

As Stephanie and Steve nodded in agreement, Aunt Michele was confused.

"What makes you say that?" Aunt Michele asked.

"The man that we met at the warehouse wasn't very friendly, and it just seemed like he was up to something," Steve said.

"Besides, we already know that the company has probably been selling their reproductions as actual antiques," Tyler said.

"But, remember, we don't know if those pieces of furniture came directly from the company," Aunt Michele pointed out. "The furniture could have switched hands several times before getting to us," Aunt Michele said.

"She's right," Tyler said. "We need to do further investigating before we come to any conclusions."

The news was over and the family was just finishing dinner when the phone rang. It was Officer Harris requesting that the teenagers and their aunt come by the station right away. The officer didn't say much over the phone, just that he needed their help.

"Did you happen to catch the news?" he asked them as they walked into his office.

"Yes, is this about the fire at the Madison Company?" Steve asked.

After the officer indicated that it was, he explained that they had a lead to follow up on. The owner of the company, Tom Dunn, had been out walking his dog when he saw smoke in the direction of his warehouse. He didn't even think of the possibility that his own warehouse was on fire. At first, he continued walking his dog. Then, he remembered an assignment that he had for a photography class; he was to take a dramatic photograph and bring it to class. Tom rushed back to his house, grabbed his camera equipment, and sped off in the direction of the fire. He was stunned when he saw that his own building was burning and was even more surprised to see strange men running from the fire. Instantly, he snapped a photo of the two men. Officer Harris handed them the picture.

"Do either of these two men look familiar?" he asked.

"It's Mr. Gomez," Steve exclaimed.

"Are you sure Steve?" the officer asked.

"Yes, I'm sure it's him, without a doubt," Steve said.

Tyler and Steve both examined the photo and agreed that one of the men was Hernandez Gomez who had sold them the furniture.

"And do you recognize the picture of Mr. Gomez?" the officer asked Aunt Michele.

"Actually, I have never met Mr. Gomez. I originally bought the furniture from one of the other employees," Aunt Michele said.

"Can you describe the person?" Officer Harris asked.

"He was a young boy with dark brown hair and he also spoke with an Hispanic accent," Aunt Michele said.

"I think that his name was Ricky," Michael said.

"That's right, it was," Aunt Michele agreed.

"Well, this is just getting more interesting," Officer Harris said. "You guys have been a big help. Thanks for coming down to the station."

"What will you do now?" Steve asked.

"First, we will try to find Mr. Gomez and the other man in the photo and bring them in for questioning. Then, we will look into this Ricky character" Officer Harris said. "By the way, if you see either of these men in the photo, please let us know right away."

"Something doesn't make sense," Tyler said, as the family was leaving the police station.

"What's that?" Stephanie asked.

"First of all, I didn't see any flames in the background of the picture but that could have been the angle of the shot. Also, I wonder why Hernandez and the other guy were still there when Mr. Dunn arrived," Tyler said.

"You're right. By the time Mr. Dunn got his camera, those guys should have been long gone," Steve said.

"You kids sure are good detectives," Aunt Michele said.

The next day, Tyler, Steve, and Stephanie decided to drive back up to the Madison Company to see if they could find any clues. At the warehouse, they soon found out that there wasn't much to go on. The fire had destroyed almost everything in the building and there wasn't any evidence of any pieces of furniture. They were going through the rubble when the man who they met before saw them.

"What are you kids doing here?" he asked, very angry.

"Are you Tom Dunn?" Steve asked the man.

"That's right, how do you know that?" he answered.

"We understand that you witnessed some men running from the building," Tyler started to say but the man wouldn't let him finish his sentence.

"You kids are probably the ones who started this fire," he accused.

"Oh, no sir. We heard about the fire on the news last night and came down here to..." Tyler started to say.

Again the man interrupted Tyler. "You kids have answers for everything."

As they were leaving, Stephanie tried to ask the man what time the fire started.

"I don't know what time it started," the man said. "I just came as fast as I could when the fire department called me."

The teenagers didn't say anything until they got in the car and were out of earshot. But they all had been thinking the same thing.

"His story sure doesn't match up. First, he accuses us of starting the fire when he's the one who has a picture of the criminals. Then, he said that he didn't know about the fire until the fire department called him," Stephanie said.

"That's not what he told the police or the reporters," Steve said.

"He is definitely up to something," Tyler said as they drove back to their aunt's house. When they arrived, the teenagers found their aunt busy in the kitchen making potato salad.

"What's up?" Stephanie asked.

"I talked to your Aunt Jennifer and she invited us up for a picnic," Aunt Michele said. "Go get your volleyball and anything else you would like to bring."

"We haven't seen Lee and Adam in a long time!" Steve said, referring to his cousins.

"Unfortunately your Uncle Lee is away on business so you won't get to see him," Aunt Michele told them.

"His map designing business sure keeps him busy," Tyler commented.

After the car was loaded, the family headed to Estes Park, where Aunt Jennifer and Uncle Lee along with their two sons, Lee and Adam, lived. The town was just outside Rocky Mountain National Park, the perfect place to go for a picnic.

Aunt Jennifer was waiting outside with Lee and Adam, who were playing catch in the front yard, when they drove up. After everyone had given each other hugs, they took two cars and headed into Rocky Mountain National Park.

"I'm applying for a job as a junior park ranger in the park for next summer," Lee told Tyler and Steve, who were in the car that Aunt Jennifer was driving.

"That's sounds like it would be a lot of fun," said Tyler, who was a year older than Lee.

There were many beautiful picnic spots in the park, and it wasn't easy to decide on where to have their picnic.

"Do you think that the area over by Sprague Lake would be a good place for a picnic?" Aunt Jennifer asked her older son.

"Sounds perfect and I'm glad we're almost there. I am starving," Lee replied.

"Yeah, that fried chicken sure makes you hungry," Steve agreed.

"Anything makes you hungry," Adam teased his cousin.

Everyone in the car laughed, as they all knew what a healthy appetite Steve had. Steve didn't bother to defend himself but made a face at his cousin.

Aunt Jennifer drove to the Sprague Lake area where she parked the car, and Aunt Michele pulled in beside her.

"There are some picnic tables down that way," she said, pointing.

The family found a picnic table that was underneath a shade tree.

"This looks like a good place," Aunt Jennifer said.

"There's plenty of food for everyone," Aunt Michele said, as she started putting the food out on the table.

Soon, everyone was full of chicken and potato salad and ready to play volleyball in a nearby clearing.

"Well, I'm worn out," Tyler said after they had played for a couple of hours.

"You mean our team wore you out," Lee teased his older cousin.

"I think everyone is tired," Aunt Jennifer said.

"Let's drive around the park and see if we can see any bighorn sheep," Aunt Michele suggested.

Bighorn sheep were often spotted in the park, and it wasn't long until the family saw a whole herd of sheep crossing the road. After admiring the sheep until they had disappeared among the rocks and trees, the family drove around the park. Then they headed back to Aunt Jennifer's house where they said goodbye and called it a day.

Everyone was up early the next morning. Aunt Michele had prepared a big breakfast of western omelets for the boys and French toast for herself and Stephanie.

"You didn't have to make French toast just for me," Stephanie said, knowing that her aunt knew she wasn't too fond of eggs.

"I made it for me, too," Aunt Michele said as she joined everyone at the table with her plate of French toast.

After breakfast Aunt Michele opened her antique store while the teenagers decided to drive down to Sandra's Antiques. They wanted to ask her about the boy who sold Aunt Michele the furniture to begin with."

"Well, I guess that's all right. But you kids better be careful," Aunt Michele said.

After the teenagers promised their aunt that they would be careful they headed down to Sandra's. They found a For Sale sign in the window of the antique store when they got there.

"Darn, I don't think anyone is here," Steve said.

They were happy to see Sandra coming from the back room after they knocked.

"Hi, kids. What's up?" she asked.

"We wanted to find out if you had a boy named Ricky working for you," Stephanie said.

"No, I just employed Mr. and Mrs. Gomez," Sandra told them.

"Our Aunt Michele said a young boy with dark hair and an Hispanic accent sold her the furniture she bought the first time she was in the store," Tyler told her.

Sandra just shook her head with a thoughtful look on her face.

"I didn't hire anyone with that description," she said. "Oh, wait a minute, you must be talking about Mr. and Mrs. Gomez's son, but he never worked for me," Sandra said. "I forgot all about Ricky. He seemed like a good kid, but I only met him once."

"So you haven't seen him lately," Tyler said.

"No, I'm sorry, I haven't," Sandra said, frowning. "And I haven't seen his lousy parents either."

"It's too bad that you have to sell your store," Stephanie said.

"What will you do?" Steve asked.

"I've decided to move to Arizona," Sandra said. "It wasn't an easy decision, though. I've been going through boxes and boxes of things and it seems like everything I have left has some kind of memory attached to it."

"That's too bad," Stephanie said.

"Well, I guess we'll let you get back to your packing then," Tyler said.

"Oh, wait a minute before you go," Sandra said. "I have some small items that you might take to your aunt since I can't use them for anything."

"That is really nice of you," Stephanie said.

"Thank you for thinking of our aunt," Tyler said, as they followed her back to her storage area where there was a pile of boxes. She handed Tyler and Steve each a small box. As the brothers were carrying the boxes out to the car, Stephanie spotted an old box of pictures that sat on a desk.

"I love old photos," she told Sandra. "Do you mind if I look through these?"

"No, not at all," Sandra said.

"Come on, Steph," Tyler called to his sister. "Let's go."

"Wait a minute, I'm looking at these old photos," Stephanie said.

"We really should get back," Tyler said.

"Tyler, Steve, come here," Stephanie said suddenly. "Look what I found."

"What is it?" Steve asked.

Sandra looked over Stephanie's shoulder. She was holding a picture of Mr. and Mrs. Gomez and their son.

"Why, that's a picture of Ricky with his parents," Sandra said.

"That's Ricky?" Tyler said astonished. "Why, that's the same boy who told us that the Gomez's sold the farm to his family!"

"That is also the boy who sold Mom the antiques to begin with," Michael said, looking over Tyler's shoulder.

Chapter 7
Strange Behavior

"You're right," Steve said. "I think I even remember the woman calling the boy Ricky."

"Can we have this picture?" Tyler asked Sandra. "It might help us catch the Gomez's."

"No problem, you can have anything you need to help your case against them," she said.

"You mean our case against them," Stephanie said, smiling.

"That's right," Sandra said, smiling back.

The teenagers said good-bye to Sandra and headed out of town toward the Gomez's farm again. They found it much like they had the last time that they were there, with several kids in the front yard playing, but Ricky and his mother didn't appear to be in sight.

One of the little girls came up to the teenagers. She was very shy and didn't say anything but just stood there.

"Ricky? Is he here?" Stephanie asked the girl.

The girl pointed to a field where the teenagers saw Ricky and his mother working. The teenagers walked over to where the two of them were working.

"We have some questions to ask you," Tyler said.

The boy looked scared and didn't say anything. The mother also looked frightened and put her arm around the boy but he shook it off, embarrassed.

"Is this you in this photo?" Tyler asked, showing him the picture.

After the boy nodded his head yes, Tyler asked him if Mr. and Mrs. Gomez were his parents.

"Parents?" Ricky said, sounding confused. "No, this is my mother, my real father died long time ago and then my Mom remarried."

"Then, how do you know the couple that you are standing with in this photo?" Tyler asked.

"They were boss," Ricky said. "I do good work for them, but they fire me."

"What happened?" Stephanie asked.

"They tell me to load furniture with Madison written on the bottom into the truck but I got mixed up and loaded the wrong furniture," he said.

"When did this happen?" Steve asked.

"It was about a couple of months ago," Ricky said.

"Did the men get you to steal the furniture back?" Tyler asked on a hunch.

"Steal? No, that would be dishonest," Ricky said, surprised. "The only furniture that I took back was not paid for."

"Do you mean that you helped your boss repossess some furniture?" Stephanie asked.

"Repossess, what does that mean?" Ricky asked, not understanding.

"When you break a promise to pay someone for something, that person can take the item back," Tyler explained.

"Right, that's what I helped them do, repossess furniture that wasn't paid for," Ricky said.

"Do you remember taking back furniture that was stored in a garage?" Tyler asked the boy.

"A couple of people had furniture stored in their garage, one was in Denver and another one was in Fort Collins," Ricky said.

"Was the garage in Fort Collins on Bear Canyon Road?" Steve asked him.

"I can't remember the exact street name but that sounds right," Ricky said. "Why?"

"That's where our aunt lives and furniture that she paid for was stolen out of her garage," Stephanie said.

"There must be some mistake," Ricky exclaimed. "I only do job. Of course, after I brought back the furniture they said they didn't need me anymore."

"That's because you already did the dirty work for them," Tyler said. "Ricky, you have to tell the police what you just told us," Tyler said.

"Tell police, oh no, I can not talk to any police," Ricky said, sounding more frightened than ever.

"These men are crooks, we need you to testify against them," Steve said.

"Sorry, no police," Ricky said. "They send us away from here."

"Oh, I see," Tyler said. "Can you tell us one more thing before we leave?"

"You can ask me another question, but I already say too much," Ricky said.

"How many people told you to sell furniture with Madison marked on it?" Tyler asked.

"There was Hernandez and his wife, Anita, but she not too happy," Ricky said. "Then, there was also Joe, and Tom."

"Tom Dunn?" Stephanie asked.

"I do not know his last name. Dark hair and brown eyes," Ricky said.

"And what does Joe look like?" Tyler asked.

"He is tall with dark brown hair, brown eyes and mustache," he answered.

"Thanks, Ricky, you've been a big help," Tyler said.

"Everything is starting to make sense," Stephanie said as the teenagers rode home.

"Yes, but Ricky can't testify or they will send him home," Tyler said.

"What do you mean?" Michael asked.

"He isn't an American citizen. That means he is in the country illegally," Tyler said.

"What about his mother?" Stephanie asked.

"She is probably here illegally as well," Tyler said. "I was thinking of going straight to Officer Harris but under the circumstances I think we should wait until we have more information.

Stephanie and Steve both agreed with their brother.

"Maybe we could help Ricky get his citizenship so he can stay in America," Stephanie said.

Arriving back at their aunt's house, they found that she'd had a busy day.

"Hi, I was just figuring out how much I made today," she said. "I sold furniture today to three different families."

"That's great news," Stephanie said.

"So how did you kids make out?" Aunt Michele asked.

After the teenagers had finished telling their Aunt about Ricky, she looked worried.

"You kids must tell Officer Harris," she said. "It's also against the law not to report knowledge of an illegal alien. We can stop by the police department on our way to dinner."

At the police department they took turns telling Officer Harris about their conversation with Ricky.

"You kids are going to have to tell me where I can find Ricky," the officer said.

"Okay, but can you at least go easy on the kid, he seems awful nice, and he is trying to be helpful," Steve said.

"I have a friend in Immigration, I'll see what I can do," Officer Harris promised.

After Tyler had written down directions to the farm where Ricky lived, the family left for dinner. They ate at one of their favorite Chinese restaurants, the Red Dragon.

"Your parents called today," Aunt Michele said after they had ordered. "They will be here on Friday."

"Did they finish the articles that they were working on?" Tyler asked.

"I guess so, they just said that they would see us in a couple of days," Aunt Michele answered.

That night the teenagers played a board game with their aunt and cousin and then made it an early night.

The next day the teenagers decided to visit Alpine Funtier, a favorite attraction in Fort Collins. At the park, there was something for all of them to do.

"Let's start with the go-karts," Steve suggested.

"Yeah, Michael can ride with me in a double seat and we'll race you," Tyler said.

Stephanie decided to get her own go-kart and stay behind while her brothers raced for the finish line. Tyler was ahead but in the end Steve sped ahead to finish first.

"I'll get you with the Lazer Tag," Tyler said, laughing.

"We'll see about that," Steve replied.

After amusing themselves with Lazer Tag, the teens decided to play a round of miniature golf. In the end, Stephanie was the winner with Michael in second place.

"I would have played better on a full stomach," Steve said.

"It sounds like someone's hungry again," Michael teased.

"Well, the poor guy hasn't eaten in three hours," Stephanie said.

"It's been longer than three hours," Steve smirked.

After lunch they decided to ride the bumper boats.

"I can't wait to ram my boat into Steve's," Tyler said.

"Oh yeah, you just wait," Steve smirked.

The boys especially had a lot of fun as they rammed their bumper boats into each other. It wasn't long until they were all soaking wet.

"I think it's time we head back," Tyler said.

"I can't wait to get out of these wet clothes," Stephanie said.

Arriving back at their aunt's house, she immediately started laughing when she saw the kids.

"It looks like you kids had fun," she said.

"It was a blast," Michael said.

After changing their clothes, the teenagers watched television while they waited for dinner. Soon dinner was on the table and, after saying grace, the family sat down to a delicious dinner that Aunt Michele had prepared.

"Why don't you kids go see a movie tonight?" Aunt Michele suggested.

"That sounds like fun," Stephanie said. "Would you like to come with us?"

"No, thanks," Aunt Michele said. "I forgot to tell you about the auction in Greeley tomorrow. It's first thing in the morning so we have to get up early."

It wasn't hard for the teenagers to decide on what movie to see. The last time they were at the movies, a new action adventure movie that they had all wanted to see had just been released. They bought some popcorn and soda, and laughed their way through the whole movie.

"I thought the car chase was hilarious," Steve said.

"The party scene was funnier," Stephanie said.

The teenagers were discussing what parts were their favorites when Tyler pulled his brother and sister aside.

"What's wrong?" Steve asked.

"Look, over there," Tyler pointed.

On the far side of the building three men were standing together talking in low voices.

"It's Mr. Gomez, Tom Dunn, and the other man must be Joe," Steve.

"It sure is," Tyler whispered. "You guys stay here, I'm going to try to hear what they are saying."

As Tyler headed toward the three men, Steve headed for the truck.

"Where are you going?" Stephanie whispered to Steve.

Steve didn't respond but just motioned to her and Michael to be quiet. When he came back, he was holding his camera. Now Stephanie knew what he was up to and helped him put on his zoom lens. He was soon snapping pictures. He had taken about four or five before the men walked off. They got in a blue sedan and drove off.

"Darn, I didn't get their license plate," Tyler said.

"That's okay, I got something better," Steve said.

"What's that?" Tyler asked.

"Smile," Steve said as he held up his camera.

"You got them on film, that's great," Tyler said. "Tom Dunn told the police that he had never seen those men before the day he saw them leave the scene of the fire, and that's just what we need to prove his story isn't true."

The next morning the teenagers were up even before their aunt. They were making breakfast together when she came downstairs.

"What are you kids doing?" she asked.

"Oh, we like making breakfast," Tyler told his aunt.

"Would you like an omelet?" Stephanie asked.

"That would be great," Aunt Michele answered. "So how was the movie last night?"

"The movie was good but you're not going to believe what happened afterwards," Stephanie said.

"That was fast thinking to grab your camera," Aunt Michele told Steve after she had heard the whole story. "Maybe your photographs will help put those three men behind bars."

After breakfast Aunt Michele didn't get objections when she insisted on doing the dishes since none of the teens liked doing dishes. She had just finished putting the dishes away when Stephanie came back into the kitchen.

"I was just thinking that you don't have to close your store. I can stay and run it while you go to the sale in Greeley," she said.

"You don't have to do that. One of the reasons I decided to open an antique store was to have control over when it was open and closed," Aunt Michele said.

"But I think the experience would be good for me, and I happen to remember at least two people who said that they might be back," Stephanie said.

"Oh, people say that all the time," her aunt replied.

"Besides, there is not room for all of us in the truck," Stephanie pointed out.

"Well, you have a point there," Aunt Michele said.

"I could stay behind and help," Steve said.

"I guess it would be all right with the two of you watching the store together," Aunt Michele said, giving in.

A couple of hours later their first customer walked in the door of Mayfair Antiques. Stephanie put down the book she was reading and asked the man if she could be of any assistance.

"I'm just browsing," the man replied.

But as Stephanie watched the man, it appeared that he was doing more than just browsing. She watched the man as he moved furniture away from the wall and crawled on his knees to look underneath the furniture. Stephanie knew that it was common for antique dealers to check items carefully but she thought that she better alert her brother.

Stephanie found him watching television in the next room and motioned to him.

"There's a man out front and he is acting strange," she whispered.

Steve joined Stephanie in the front of the store where they found the man moving furniture.

"Don't you have any reproductions?" he asked, barely looking up at them.

"Sorry, we only sell genuine antiques," Stephanie said.

"What about the furniture from Sandra's..." the man started to say but didn't finish his sentence. "Never mind, I guess I'll try somewhere else."

As the man left the store, the twins looked at each other. How did the man know about the reproductions from Sandra's Antiques?

∼

Chapter 8
Missing

"He just asked us about the reproductions that we got from Sandra's Antiques," Stephanie said.

"The question is, how does he know about the reproductions and why would he want to buy them?" Steve said.

While the twins were trying to figure this out, Aunt Michele was looking through the items at the auction to decide which ones to bid on.

"I like this desk but it'll probably go for more than I want to pay," she said, examining it.

It wasn't long before the auctioneer officially started the auction. The first item for bid was an antique grandfather clock. It wasn't until several items later that Aunt Michele started bidding on furniture. She was in the middle of bidding on a china cabinet when suddenly a woman yelled out in the crowd.

"That cabinet is stolen!" the woman accused.

The crowd went completely silent as the woman and her husband went to the front where the auctioneer was standing.

"What do you mean this piece of furniture is stolen?" he asked.

"My husband and I put this china cabinet on layaway months ago at Sandra's Antiques," the woman said.

As the woman mentioned the name Sandra's Antiques, the crowd went crazy. Many people started to recognize items that could possibly be the same ones that they too had put away on layaway at the antique store.

"That table looks very similar to what we had put on layaway at the antique store," one of the women said.

"I don't know why I didn't recognize that dresser sooner," another said.

As the auctioneer tried to calm down the crowd, Tyler went to call Officer Harris, who wasn't in. He told the dispatcher the address of the auction and said if it was at all possible to have him come by. When he returned to the angry crowd, Aunt Michele was explaining to the crowd that it wasn't the owner's fault but most of them didn't believe her.

"The owner knew nothing about what was going on?" a man asked.

"If she was in on these people's little scheme, why would she refund my money?" Aunt Michele answered.

As soon as she said the word refund, several people rushed out the door in hopes that they too might get a refund. As they were leaving, Officer Harris pulled up in his police car. Tyler explained to the officer what had happened and after the auctioneer joined them, they decided the auction should be postponed until they could investigate.

"It's terrible how so many people got hurt in this mess," Aunt Michele said, as they drove home.

Tyler and Michael were full of excitement when they got back to their aunt's house.

"You guys are not going to believe what happened at the auction," Tyler said.

"You won't believe what happened here either," Stephanie said.

After Tyler told his brother and sister about the events at the estate sale, the twins took turns telling them about the man who had come into the store.

"What did this man look like?" Tyler asked when they were done.

"He was tall with brown eyes, dark brown hair, and a mustache," Stephanie said.

"Come to think of it, he did look a little familiar," Steve said.

"Could it have been Tom Dunn's partner, Joe?" Tyler asked them.

"Yes, it did look like him but why would a partner from the Madison Company buy their own furniture back?" Stephanie asked.

"It doesn't make any sense to me either," Tyler said.

"It does seem very strange," Aunt Michele agreed as she started to unload the groceries that she had bought to make dinner that night. "Your mom and dad will be here soon so I'd better get started on dinner."

"Do you need any help?" Stephanie asked.

"No, thanks," Aunt Michele said. "I am just making a meatloaf and a salad."

While Aunt Michele was busy making dinner, Tyler pulled his brother and sister aside.

"It seems like we are just starting to piece together this mystery," he said.

"And now it's almost time to go home," Steve said, picking up on his brother's train of thought. "Since school is still three weeks away, maybe we can stay longer."

"Especially if Aunt Michele invited us to stay longer," Stephanie said and then added, "I think I'll check to see how dinner is coming."

A few minutes later, Stephanie joined her brothers, who were in the living room playing checkers.

"Guess what," she said, with a grin.

"Aunt Michele has asked if we want to stay longer," Tyler said, smiling.

"How in the world did you guess that?" Stephanie asked, smiling back.

Just then the doorbell rang, and the teenagers rushed to it, knowing it was their parents.

"Oops, we must have the wrong house," Jack Thompson teased when Steve opened the door.

"Good luck finding the right house," Steve teased back and started to close the door but was unable to close it as his father pushed the door open.

As the family exchanged hugs, Aunt Michele joined them and said that dinner was ready.

"You're just in time," she said. "A few minutes later and Steve would have eaten your share."

"Why is everyone picking on me?" Steve said.

"Oh, poor baby," Stephanie teased.

"That's enough joking around, tell us what have you kids been doing," Carol Thompson said.

While the family ate dinner, the teenagers all took turns filling their parents in on all of the events that had taken place.

"It sounds like you kids are figuring out all of the details to solve this mystery," their father said.

"Speaking of details, Steve we still need to get your film developed," Tyler said.

"That's right, the picture will show that Tom Dunn lied to the police," Steve said.

"You can do that tomorrow morning," Jack Thompson said. "I thought we could spend some family time together tonight. What would you kids like to do?"

After going through several options, everyone finally agreed on playing putt-putt golf.

"Aunt Michele has invited us to stay for a few more days," Stephanie said as they arrived at the amusement park.

"Oh, I don't know," Carol Thompson said. "We do have to get ready for school."

"Mom, it's three weeks away," Steve said.

"I guess it's okay," their mother said.

"Are you sure, it's all right with you, Sis?" Jack asked his sister.

"Oh, sure, the kids have been a big help to me," she answered. "They haven't had much of a summer, though."

"Sure, we have," Tyler said. "We're just not ready to let it end."

After playing a couple games of putt-putt golf, the family headed back to Aunt Michele's where the kids handed their parents their anniversary gifts. Both of their parents looked surprised.

"You thought we forgot, didn't you?" Stephanie said.

"I was wondering if you remembered that it was our anniversary," their mother said.

"It was nice of you to remember, but you didn't have to get us presents," their father added.

Jack and Carol Thompson opened their anniversary gifts from their children.

"I love all of them," Carol Thompson said, hugging each of them.

"Yes, thanks, kids," Jack said. "I think I'm ready for bed now."

"Oh no, you're not done yet," Aunt Michele said. "You're not getting away that easy."

As Tyler carried his aunt's gift into the room, his mother looked at the large, wrapped gift, astonished.

"Well, what on earth could it be?" she said.

"We'll soon find out," Jack Thompson said. "Let's tear the wrapping paper off together."

When they saw the beautiful carved eagle, they were both speechless.

"Why, we have been looking for something just like this for our flower garden," Carol Thompson said. "Thank you so much, it was so thoughtful."

"Yes, thanks, Sis," Jack Thompson added. "You're the greatest."

"Well, I try," Aunt Michele said, smiling.

The next morning after the teenagers said goodbye to their parents, they headed to the local drug store to get their film developed. They browsed for an hour at the store while the film was being processed. After they got the film back, they soon learned that Steve had captured a perfect view of the three men. They wasted no time in getting it to the Boulder Police Department. Officer Harris was really impressed with the photo.

"You're right, this is very suspicious," he said. "And it backs up what Ricky told me."

"So, how did it go with Ricky?" Tyler asked.

"I have good news," Officer Harris said. "He didn't realize that when his mother became a U.S. citizen by marrying an American, that made him one too."

"That's wonderful!" Steve said. "He really seems like a terrific kid."

"Yeah, he's so terrific that he has agreed to help us solve this case," Officer Harris said. "He thinks he might know where these three men are hiding and is going to go back to them and ask them to give him some more work."

"Isn't that dangerous?" Stephanie asked.

"We only need a little more information," Officer Harris said. "I have to go on patrol but not a word about this to anyone or it might slip out that we are on to these men and then it could get dangerous."

"You have our word," Tyler said as they said good-bye.

After thanking the officer the teenagers headed to the library where they researched schools in the area that offered photography courses.

"Now we just need to call these schools and see if a Tom Dunn is registered," Stephanie said.

But they soon found out that was easier said than done. As they started calling the schools, they found out that they were asking for privileged information that could not be given out over the phone.

"Well, that's a dead-end," Steve said.

"I don't think that the police believe the story that Tom Dunn rushed to the fire to take pictures for his photography class anyway," Tyler said.

"I think you're right," Stephanie said. "Let's go tell Aunt Michele what Officer Harris told us."

When the teenagers walked into their aunt's antique store, they found their aunt working on a crossword puzzle.

"That's great news," Aunt Michele said after they told her how close the police were to putting the crooks in jail. "Now maybe you kids can enjoy what's left of your summer vacation."

"Yeah, I was thinking that it would be fun to go on one last camping trip before the end of the summer." Tyler said.

"That sounds like fun," Steve agreed.

"Can I go with them?" Michael asked his mother.

"I don't see why not. There are several campgrounds near here along the Cache la Poudre River," Aunt Michele said.

"The only problem is that all of our camping gear is at home," Tyler said.

"Well, you can rent a tent, and I bet that we can find anything else you might need," Aunt Michele said.

"That's a good idea," Tyler said. "I do remember seeing a rental place not far from here; we can check it out after lunch."

While Aunt Michele got lunch ready, the teenagers put together some blankets that they could use as sleeping bags, some of their aunt's old cookware and utensils, a couple of flashlights, a radio, and even a couple of fishing poles.

"That should be about it," Steve said as their aunt called them to lunch.

After lunch the kids headed to the rental place where they found several tents available to rent. After picking one out, the teenagers then headed northwest to the area that their aunt had suggested to locate a campground. Just like their aunt had said, they saw several along the river. After visiting a couple different campgrounds, they finally decided on Red Feather Campground.

"This campground is perfect," Tyler said. "We can even arrange to go white water rafting along the Cache la Poudre River."

"That sounds like fun," Michael agreed.

"Well, while the two of you are doing that, Stephanie and I will be fishing," Steve said.

"Fine with us," Tyler said.

On the way back to Aunt Michele's house, the group stopped to buy some extra camping supplies.

"We definitely need some lures," Steve said.

"And bait," Stephanie added.

"Maybe we should get some spinners," Steve suggested.

"I'm going to get some batteries while you guys are picking out the fishing supplies," Tyler told them.

"I'll come with you," Michael said.

When the two of them came back several minutes later, they had a pile of snack food in their cart.

"You call those batteries?" Stephanie asked.

"Snack power," Michael said, smiling.

Back at Aunt Michele's house, the teenagers played a board game while their aunt was getting dinner ready. After dinner they sat down to watch some television but could not agree on what to watch.

"I don't really feel like watching television," Steve said.

"Me either, we should go do something, like roller-skating," Stephanie said.

"There is a rink only a few blocks from here," Aunt Michele said. "You should give them a call and find out what they have going on tonight."

"I think I'll stay here tonight and read," Tyler said after Stephanie called to find out that there was a teen skate that night.

Tyler drove his siblings and his cousin to the skating rink and told them to call when they were ready to be picked up. It was an hour later when the phone rang.

"Steve, don't tell me you're ready to come back already?" Tyler said teasingly.

"No, turn on Channel 9 News quick!" Steve said.

The police department was seeking community involvement to help them locate a missing boy. Tyler listened as the media described the boy as a sixteen-year old Hispanic boy. The news then showed a picture of the boy, making Tyler gasp. It was Ricky!

~

Chapter 9
Clue Found

Tyler listened closely to the news story but the report didn't give much information.

"What happened?" Aunt Michele asked as she entered the room.

"Apparently, Ricky hasn't been home in two days so his mother reported him missing to the police," Tyler said.

"They didn't give any more information?" Aunt Michele asked.

"Nope, but I would bet anything that Tom Dunn and Hernandez Gomez have something to do with this," Tyler said. "I'm going to pick up Michael, Steve, and Stephanie; they don't feel like skating anymore."

The twins and their cousin were sitting outside the skating rink on the steps when Tyler pulled up.

"The manager turned the channel on the television set right after we hung up with you," Steve told his brother. "Did the media give any more information?"

"Nothing at all," Tyler said. "I bet the police are very worried about him, since they basically asked Ricky to play spy."

"Yeah, maybe the men caught Ricky spying on them," Stephanie said.

"That's a good possibility," Tyler replied.

That night the Thompson kids were all down in the dumps. Their camping trip had been planned for the next day but it didn't sound like fun anymore.

"Canceling your camping trip isn't going to help the police find Ricky any faster," Aunt Michele said.

"Aunt Michele is right, "Tyler said. "Let's get some sleep, we're going camping tomorrow."

The next morning after breakfast, the teenagers loaded the truck with their camping supplies and said good-bye to Aunt Michele.

"Have fun and don't you worry about Ricky, the police will find him," she said.

As Tyler started his father's truck, he told the others his idea.

"I was thinking that we could at least make a detour to Ricky's house and find out if his mother can help fill in the details," Tyler said.

"That's a great idea," Stephanie said.

Reaching the farm where Ricky lived with his family, it appeared that the place was deserted. They called out but no one answered. Tyler knocked on the door to the house. Thinking that no one was home, they were about to leave when Ricky's mom came to the door. She spoke mostly in Spanish with only a little broken English.

"We know this must be really hard for you," Tyler said. "But we would like to ask you a few questions."

"I don't know much. Ricky go to work but never come home," she said.

"Do you know where he was working?" Steve asked.

"He just say, port," she said.

Tyler tried asking the woman if she knew where this port was but she didn't understand what he was asking, and was too upset to figure it out.

"Oh, help me find my boy," she said.

"We'll do our best," Tyler promised.

The teenagers thanked the woman and headed for their campground. On the way, they discussed where the "port" could be.

"There are no ports around here," Steve said.

"Do you think he could have gone to another state somewhere on a shoreline?" Stephanie asked.

"It's possible, but from what little English his mother knows, she could have gotten the word wrong," Tyler said.

The group was so involved in their discussion that they almost missed the turnoff for their campground.

"Hey, didn't that sign say to take a left up here to go to Rustic?" Steve asked his brother.

"That's right. Thanks, I almost missed it." Tyler said.

Reaching the campground the teenagers picked out a site and set up their camp. As soon as they were done, they tried catching some fish to cook for dinner. The new lures that they had bought worked well and after fishing for only an hour, the first fish was caught.

"I got a bite," Tyler said.

He gave the line a small jerk then he slowly reeled the fish in to find that he had caught about an eight-pound rainbow trout.

He had no sooner taken his fish off the hook when Steve said that he thought he felt a nibble on his line. He was soon reeling in another rainbow trout that was just a little smaller than Tyler's.

"You guys are lucky," Michael said.

"These new lures work well," Tyler said.

The teenagers continued fishing for another hour before deciding to head back to camp and cook Tyler's and Steve's fish. After dinner they went on a hike through the woods. They were used to hiking and knew to mark their trail so that they could find their way back. Along their hike they saw that another trail had been marked.

"I wonder where this goes," Stephanie said.

"Let's find out," Steve said.

They followed the trail a long way to discover that the markers just stopped in the middle of the woods. They decided to walk a little farther to see if the markers appeared again but found nothing.

"Oh, well, the markers are probably really old," Stephanie said.

But as they walked back to where the trail had ended, Steve noticed something up in the trees.

"Look! It's a tree house," he said.

"That's why the markers stopped," Stephanie said.

Steve called up to the tree house to see if anyone was up there but got no reply.

"Let's go up," he suggested.

Reaching the tree house the teenagers didn't find much. On the floor there were some mats to sit on, a small handmade table, and a pair of binoculars. There was also a gap in the wood that gave them a perfect view of the lake below.

"You can see almost to the other side of the lake from up here," Stephanie said.

"You can see even better with these," Steve said, as he picked up the binoculars and looked out the gap in the wall.

The teenagers took turns using the binoculars before climbing down from the tree house.

"I wonder who has been using the tree house," Stephanie said.

"We should ask the owners of the campground," Tyler said.

They all agreed and found the owners, who were sitting by their own campfire. The owners explained that their grandkids had built the tree house years ago.

"I like to go up there myself and watch for animals," the husband said.

"So the binoculars belong to you?" Tyler asked.

"Yes," he replied and then he added, "You kids can use them if you want; you can see a long way with them."

After thanking the owners, they went back to camp where they started a fire and roasted some marshmallows. Then they took turns telling ghost stories. Steve was trying to retell a story that he had read over the summer but he couldn't seem to remember how it went.

"That makes no sense," Stephanie teased him.

"Well, it went something like that," Steve said.

The teenagers were laughing so hard that their laughter echoed throughout the camp. Tyler decided to scare his brother and sister.

"Be quiet," he whispered as he gave a wink to Michael so he wouldn't scare him. "I think I heard something."

Everyone stopped talking and listened but all that they could hear was the wind whistling through the trees.

"I know I heard something," he said.

"Tyler, I don't hear anything," Stephanie said. "And the only lights I see are over there, flickering off and on."

"It looks like some kid is playing around with a flashlight," Steve said.

"I bet Steve is right, there is probably another camp on the other side of the lake," Michael said.

The teenagers watched the lights flickering off and on for some time but then they just died out.

"Let's get some sleep," Tyler said. "Tomorrow we will try to figure out where the flashing lights were coming from."

The next morning right after breakfast the teenagers decided to go on a hike through the woods.

"Let's walk in the direction of the tree house," Stephanie suggested.

The tree house wasn't very far from camp, and when they reached it, they each climbed to the top. They were disappointed that they didn't see any animals around.

"Oh, well," Tyler said. "What do you guys want to do today?"

"There are stables down the road from here. Why don't we rent some horses?" Stephanie suggested.

Her brothers were quick to agree with her. They lived down the road from some stables, but they didn't have many chances to go riding since they spent most of their summer away from home.

"I've never been on a horse," Michael said shyly.

"It's a lot of fun and real easy," Steve said.

"Yeah, the horses are well trained, and they do all the work," Stephanie said.

"It does sound like fun," Michael agreed.

They rode for several hours until Tyler said it was time to get the horses back to the stable. They were riding back when Tyler realized that they had gotten turned around.

"Don't we go this way?" Steve asked.

"No, I'm pretty sure it's this way," Tyler said.

"Oh, great. Now we are lost," Stephanie said. "It looks like there is a sign up the road, let's ride up and see what it says."

"The sign looks really old but it looks like it says, 'Colona - 20 miles'," Steve said.

"That town name doesn't sound familiar, we better head back this way," Tyler suggested.

As they rode in the opposite direction, they soon saw a sign for Rustic and knew where they were.

"At least I know we're going in the right direction now," Tyler said.

They were all hungry by the time they reached camp and heated up some stew that their Aunt Michele had made for them. Afterwards they played a game of cards in their tent.

"I wonder if we'll see the flickering lights again tonight," Steve said.

But that night the teenagers sat at the edge of the lake skipping rocks and all was quiet and dark.

When Stephanie woke up early the next morning she tried waking her brothers up.

"It's too early to get up," Steve said. "We have to sleep in while we still can; after all, school will be starting in only a couple of weeks."

Stephanie rolled over and tried to go back to sleep knowing that her brother was right, but she couldn't get back to sleep. After lying there several minutes, she decided to go for a walk along the lake. She was enjoying her early morning stroll when she suddenly stepped on something and stubbed her toe.

"Ouch," she said, looking down to see what she had stepped on.

Stephanie had stubbed her toe on a branch that was sticking out of the ground. But while she stopped to rest her toe, she spotted a gold-colored object next to the piece of wood. As she picked it up, she was startled by her brother as he came up behind her.

"What did you find?" he asked.

"Steve, you made me jump," Stephanie said. "What are you doing up?"

"I couldn't go back to sleep so I decided to see what you were doing," Steve said.

"I stubbed my toe on a piece of wood and found this old key," Stephanie said.

Steve looked at the key his sister had found. "It says something but most of it looks rubbed off."

"Let me look at it again," Stephanie said. "It looks like it says Colona, CO."

"That's the same name that was on the sign that we saw," Steve said. "It must be a town around here."

Back at camp the twins found Tyler and Michael sitting by the fire ring. Tyler was making breakfast.

"Look what we found," Stephanie said, showing him the key.

"Where did you find it?" he asked.

"Down by the lake close to the boat ramp," Stephanie said.

"Well, someone must have dropped it getting into a boat," Tyler said.

"Check out what is inscribed on the key," Steve said, showing his brother the inscription.

"Colona, CO.?" Tyler read aloud. "That's the same name as the sign but I still don't remember any towns by that name. I'll have to check the map later."

After breakfast the teenagers decided to go on another hike through the woods. Coming to the tree house, they decided to climb up and found that nothing had changed since their last visit.

"I do wonder what's on the other side of the lake," Steve said as he looked across the lake with the binoculars that had been left there.

"We were on that side of the lake when we went horseback riding," Tyler said. "I bet the town of Colona is near there."

"I know the names of just about every town around here but I don't remember any by that name," Michael said.

"We'll look at the map when we get back to camp," Tyler said.

The teenagers continued their hike through the woods where they came upon a herd of deer.

"Darn, I forgot my camera back at the campsite," Steve whispered trying not to scare the deer.

The teenagers watched the deer, which looked up at them and then ran off in the other direction. After hiking a little farther, they decided to head back to camp for lunch.

"We can warm up the beef stew that Aunt Michele made for us," Stephanie said as she started a fire.

Steve helped his sister while Tyler got out a map of Colorado and looked up the town Colona.

"There isn't any town by that name on this map," he told the others.

"The sign looked really old, it could be a name of a town that has since changed its name," Stephanie suggested.

"We can check that old map that Aunt Marybeth gave us in Manitou Springs and see if we find the name Colona," Tyler suggested.

"That's a great idea!" Steve said.

"I think the map is still in the glove compartment," Stephanie said as she went to get it.

"Bingo!" Tyler said, smiling as he read through the list of towns. "It looks like the town is now named Laporte."

"The stew is warmed up," Stephanie told the others as she started dishing it out.

Steve was the first to get his, but as he started to eat, he was still thinking about what Tyler had just said.

"I don't know why that name, Laporte, sounds so familiar...," he started to say but just then they all realized the same thing.

Ricky's mom said that he went to the port! Could she have meant Laporte?

Chapter 10
The Last Signal

The teenagers knew that it was probably a coincidence but they all agreed that they had to investigate.

"Laporte is also in the direction where we saw the flashing light from the tree house," Steve reminded them.

"That's right!" Tyler said.

"Maybe the flashing light was Ricky signaling for help," Stephanie said.

The teenagers decided to drive over to the other side of the lake to the town of Laporte. There, they hoped to locate where the flashing lights were coming from.

"I think I see a small cabin up that way," Steve said, pointing through the trees.

Tyler stopped the truck and the teenagers quietly started walking up to the cabin. They didn't get far before a dog started barking.

"We better get out of here before we're discovered," Tyler said.

"That was close," Stephanie said back at the truck.

"We had better just wait until tonight," Steve added.

After swimming, mountain biking, and a few card games, sundown was approaching. Because they didn't feel like bothering with a campfire and taking the time to make sure the fire was completely out, the teenagers went to a nearby restaurant for dinner. While they were eating, a dark-haired man came in to pick up a take-out order.

"Hey, this isn't right," the man complained.

"Sorry, that's the order we took," the cashier said.

"Well, it's all wrong and I expect you to change it," the man said, his voice getting louder and louder.

"Certainly sir, but it will take a few minutes to change it," the cashier said.

"I'll wait," he said.

"I think that's the same man who came in Aunt Michele's store asking for reproductions," Steve said.

"It sure does look like him," Stephanie agreed.

"I'll follow him when he leaves," Tyler whispered. "You guys better stay here just in case anything happens. If I'm not back in an hour, call Officer Harris."

Tyler trailed the man in his father's pickup into the town of Laporte without being noticed. When the man turned off the main road onto a rural side road, Tyler decided not to take his chances and follow the man any farther. It was the same road that the teenagers had been on earlier, and he already knew where it led, to the small cabin down by the lake.

"I think our guess was right," Tyler said when he returned. "He went right back to that cabin."

"What we have to figure out is if they have Ricky in that cabin," Steve said. "But how can we investigate without getting kidnapped ourselves?"

"I have a plan," Tyler said after several minutes. "We'll wait to see if there are any signals from across the lake. If it is Ricky and he is able to signal then he is probably alone so we would have a good opportunity to rescue him."

"But it will take us too long to reach Ricky across the lake after he signals," Stephanie said.

"That's a good point," Steve said.

"You guys can watch for Ricky's signal while I hide out near the cabin," Tyler said. "When Ricky signals, you guys can signal to me to let me know it is safe to proceed."

"That's a good idea," Michael said.

As nightfall approached the teenagers sat in the dark, waiting for the light signals to come from across the lake. When they appeared Steve turned his flashlight on and off, signaling to Tyler.

"I hope he is careful," Stephanie said.

Meanwhile, as Tyler neared the cabin, he heard some voices. He stopped in his tracks and listened carefully.

"Tom, he's only a kid," one of the voices said.

"A kid who is going to land all of us in jail," another voice said.

Tyler hid in the bushes nearby, holding his breath. He knew that if the men found him, he would become their next kidnapping victim. Luckily, the voices faded as the men moved in the opposite direction. After overhearing the conversation, he knew that he had located Ricky, but could he rescue him? He had only heard two voices, which probably meant that the third man was watching over him. But if it wasn't safe to approach, what were the flashing signals for? Tyler decided to take his chances and slowly moved closer to the cabin. He was glad that he did when he saw Ricky looking out the window.

"Ricky! Are you all right?" Tyler asked.

"Shh," Ricky said. He then pulled back the drape to show Joe who apparently was supposed to be guarding him but had fallen asleep.

"Let's get you out of here," Tyler whispered.

"My legs are tied to the chair," Ricky whispered.

Tyler knew what he had to do. He had to go into the cabin and untie the rope around Ricky's legs, and he had to do it without waking Joe. He took a deep breath and entered the cabin.

Inside he quietly tried to untie Ricky but the knots were really tight. He worked them with his fingers until they started to loosen up. But he had only gotten one knot loose when he suddenly heard voices. The voices were getting closer.

"Hide!" Ricky whispered.

"What?" said the man who had been sleeping and was starting to wake up.

Tyler quickly slid underneath a bed nearby and the men entered the cabin.

"Joe, did you fall asleep again?" one of them said.

"No," he started to say.

"Yeah, you did!" a voice said. "Look Tom, the kid has loosened his knots!"

"We'll fix that!" the other voice said.

"Just great," thought Tyler. "Now I am trapped."

Meanwhile back at camp, Steve, Stephanie, and Michael were all getting nervous.

"Tyler was supposed to signal to us if he was able to rescue Ricky," Stephanie said.

"He could have gotten caught," Michael said.

"There is no reason to panic," Steve said, trying to think of what his older brother would do.

"If we don't hear from him in half-an-hour, we'll call Officer Harris," he said.

It was almost half-an-hour when Stephanie said, "I can't stand this anymore, let's go call Officer Harris."

Steve quickly agreed with his sister and the trio went to a nearby pay phone at the campground. Stephanie pulled the officer's number out of her pocket.

"I'll call," Steve offered.

Steve explained the situation to the officer who said he would be right out.

While the others were waiting for the officer, Tyler was listening to the conversation in the cabin. Ricky was getting the men to admit to counterfeiting furniture so Tyler could hear.

"You think you fool everyone buying reproductions from Madison Company and selling them as real antiques?" Ricky asked.

"We had a brilliant plan, and it was working fine," one of them said. "That is until you and those nosy friends of yours came along."

"And then Tom started that fire and tried to blame us," another said.

"I figured that you guys had already given yourselves away," the voice that Tyler now knew as Tom Dunn said. "I mean what was the point of going into the antique stores looking to buy back the reproductions?"

"We didn't want to buy back the furniture, stupid," one of them said.

"Yeah, we just wanted to find out if they knew the pieces were fakes," another said.

"And did you ever think that they might examine the pieces closer if they hadn't already figured it out?" Tom asked.

"Oh, it doesn't matter now anyway," one of them said. "We'll have the insurance money any day now. Then after we each get our share, we can split it and never have to see each other again."

"Sounds good to me," Tom said.

"Yeah, I don't care if I ever see..." one of them started to say. "Shh, I heard a noise outside," a voice said. "Joe, go check it out."

Joe left the cabin and was gone for several minutes.

"Well, what's taking so long?" a voice said. "I'll go have a look."

The third man grumbled as he waited for the two men.

"What is taking them so..." he started to say to himself, when all of a sudden his thought was interrupted.

"Hold it right there!" Two police officers stormed into the room.

The police had completely caught the man off guard and had him cornered.

"Put your hands up!" Officer Harris ordered.

Once the police had him handcuffed, Tyler came out from underneath the bed.

"What the...?" the man started to say but again he was interrupted as Officer Harris read him his rights.

"Tyler, Ricky, are you both all right?" Stephanie asked.

"We're both fine," Tyler answered. "Did you guys get the other two men as they came out of the cabin?"

"Sure did, one by one," Officer Harris said. "Tyler, you were really lucky that you didn't get caught."

"I know, it was real close," Tyler said. "I was starting to get Ricky untied when the men returned to the cabin."

During the drive back to Aunt Michele's, the teenagers were full of excitement.

"We did a good job solving this case," Stephanie said.

"After we figured out Laporte, it was easy," Tyler said.

It was late by the time they reached their aunt's house and she had already gone to bed. Even though they couldn't wait to tell her the news, they decided not to wake her up.

"Guess what happened last night!" Steve exclaimed.

"It turns out Ricky was in that cabin like we thought and signaling for help. Tyler found him and tried to rescue him but the men came back and he had to hide underneath the bed."

"What!" Aunt Michele said. "Tyler, why did you try to rescue him by yourself?"

"The others knew where I was so they could phone for help," Tyler said.

After breakfast the family visited Ricky and his mother on their farm.

"Gracias," Ricky's mother kept saying.

"You're welcome," Tyler said. "We were glad to help."

"You were a big help to me also," Aunt Michele said. "I don't know how to thank you."

"Just sell lots of antiques," Stephanie said.

"And come visit us," Steve added.

The family headed back to Aunt Michele's house where the kids packed up all of their belongings.

"We are going to really miss you kids being around," Aunt Michele said.

"Yeah, we will miss you too," Steve said. "I have to admit, though, I can't wait to see Andrew."

"It will be great to see Kamryn," Stephanie said.

All three teenagers, who usually spent a lot of time with their best friends, talked about what activities they would do with them as the family headed home to Buena Vista. They only had a few days of summer vacation left.

"I'm not looking forward to going back to school, but it'll be nice just to have a simple school routine," Steve said.

But from the very first day of school, they would quickly realize that it wasn't going to be a typical school year. The teens would soon be trying to solve the case of The Runaway Vandals.

~

A Brief History
of LaPorte and Fort Collins, Colorado

LaPorte, which means "the gate" in French, was named by early trappers who settled in the area as early as 1828. The trappers saw the region, which is located north of the South Platte River, as the gateway to the mountains. LaPorte quickly grew, as hunters and trappers made it their home along with Arapahoe Indians, who had peacefully settled there. LaPorte was also home of the first permanent white settler, Antoine Janis, who settled there in 1844. Kit Carson brought his company of trappers to the area in 1849, and they set up camp along the Cache la Poudre River.

In 1860 LaPorte became a town, but it was originally called Colona. It was here that fifty to sixty homes were established along the river. In 1861 Colona became the first county seat of Larimer County. The name was changed to LaPorte in 1862 and it was soon a booming town with stage coaches and wagon trains often passing through the area. The town had two blacksmith shops, a butcher shop, a hotel, four saloons, and a very prosperous general store.

LaPorte also became the headquarters of the Mountain Division of the Overland Trail Stage Route. The station was built along the Cache la Poudre River and the first bridge over the river was a toll bridge widely used by prospectors heading to California.

Because LaPorte was the most important settlement north of Denver, the 9th Kansas Volunteer Cavalry built Camp Collins to protect the Cherokee trail and protect the Overland Stage Line. A couple of years later a major flood covered the camp and soldiers had to seek higher ground. Colonel Collins inspected the area and on August 20, 1864, he signed the order to move Camp Collins to present day Fort Collins. Fort Collins celebrates this day as its birthday. A couple of months after the camp moved, the name was changed from Camp to Fort Collins but there seems to be no explanation for the name change.

Fort Collins remained a military post for almost two years and then it was abandoned. Only one building from the old fort, a cabin where Auntie Elizabeth Stone lived, has been preserved. Auntie Stone was the first white woman to be a permanent residence of Fort Collins. In 1873 Fort Collins was officially incorporated as a town and, when the Colorado Central Railroad arrived in 1877, it became a thriving farming community. In 1879 the Agricultural College of Colorado was opened with only five students in attendance. The school was later named Colorado State University and today is a highly respected school.

How many books have you read in the Rocky Mountain Mystery series?

<u>Mystery on Rampart Hill</u> is the first book in this exciting new series. Follow the Thompson kids as they investigate rumors that an old house, which is being restored into a library, is haunted. Who is the man snooping around the house, and why is he trying to scare them away? Does he have something to hide? Their detective work leads to more questions and despite receiving a warning note, they are determined to get some answers so that they can enjoy their new library.

<u>Manitou Art Caper</u> is the second book in this series, and you will find that it is full of adventure. The teenagers are visiting their aunt in Manitou Springs where several art galleries have been robbed. They investigate the robberies and as they discover clues, the teenagers wonder if their new friend's uncle could be guilty. But would the real thief leave so many clues behind? Maybe he is being set up. Read the book to find out if the teen detectives can find the real robbers and prove that their friend's uncle is innocent.

What is next to come in the series? Here is a little hint.

<u>The Runaway Vandals</u> will be the fourth book in the series. Watch for its arrival as you will want to find out how the teenagers track down who is vandalizing their school and causing all kinds of mischief.

For more information about the series and to find out what's coming next, check out our website:

www.RockyMountainMysteries.com

Autobiography of Emily Burns

Emily Burns was only four years old the first time she saw the Rocky Mountains and fell in love with them. Growing up in Ohio, she dreamed that someday she would make her home in the mountains, and as she grew up, she realized another passion: writing. Even as a young child, she could often be found in some hidden corner writing or reading.

Having spent a lot of time with children, including work as a nanny, Emily has come to realize that writing for children is an area that comes naturally for her. In particular, she excels in writing mysteries for juveniles, which is still her favorite reading material even as an adult.

Today, she resides in Aurora, Colorado, just east of the mountains, with her daughter and husband.

Artist Bio

John Breeding is a talented young artist currently studying fine arts at his high school in Colorado. His artwork has appeared in many art shows, and he has received the Outstanding Young Authors and Illustrators Award. His plans for the future include college and a career in art.

Give the Gift of
Rocky Mountain Mysteries™
to your children, relatives, friends, or anyone with kids 8-12 years old
Check Your Local Bookstore or Order Here

☐ *Mystery on Rampart Hill* _____ x $4.95 = _____

☐ *Manitou Art Caper* _____ x $4.95 = _____

☐ *Marked Evidence* _____ x $4.95 = _____

Add $2.00 shipping for one book
plus $1.00 for each additional book = _____

CO Residents add
.18¢ sales tax per book = _____

Total Enclosed = _____
U.S. Funds Only
Please allow up to six (6) weeks for delivery

Name _____

Address _____

City _____ State _____ Zip _____

Phone _____

Email Address _____

Parents:
Fill out to pay by Credit Card or Order online at
www.RockyMountainMysteries.com

Please circle one [MasterCard] [VISA]

CC Number _____ Exp Date _____

Authorized Name _____

Signature _____

Make Checks or Money Orders payable and mail to:
Covered Wagon Publishing, LLC
P.O. Box 473038
Aurora, CO 80047
(303) 751-0992 Fax (303) 632-6794

Give the Gift of
Rocky Mountain Mysteries™
to your children, relatives, friends, or anyone with kids 8-12 years old
Check Your Local Bookstore or Order Here

☐ *Mystery on Rampart Hill* _____ x $4.95 = _____

☐ *Manitou Art Caper* _____ x $4.95 = _____

☐ *Marked Evidence* _____ x $4.95 = _____

Add $2.00 shipping for one book
plus $1.00 for each additional book = _____

CO Residents add
.18¢ sales tax per book = _____

Total Enclosed = _____
U.S. Funds Only
Please allow up to six (6) weeks for delivery

Name _____

Address _____

City _____ State _____ Zip _____

Phone _____

Email Address _____

Parents:
Fill out to pay by Credit Card or Order online at
www.RockyMountainMysteries.com

Please circle one MasterCard VISA

CC Number _____ Exp Date _____

Authorized Name _____

Signature _____

Make Checks or Money Orders payable and mail to:
Covered Wagon Publishing, LLC
P.O. Box 473038
Aurora, CO 80047
(303) 751-0992 Fax (303) 632-6794